Wylder Sins

by

L. M. Gonzalez

The Wylder West

Wylder Sins

Cover Art by *Tina Lynn Stout*

The Wild Rose Press, Inc.
PO Box 708
Adams Basin, NY 14410-0708
Visit us at www.thewildrosepress.com

Publishing History
First Edition, 2023
Trade Paperback ISBN 978-1-5092-4816-2
Digital ISBN 978-1-5092-4817-9

The Wylder West
Published in the United States of America

"I want to kiss you, Lina," he said.

Her heart traveled to her throat, and she couldn't speak.

Jack opened his legs and pulled her close. "Lean down and let me kiss you, darling."

Lina couldn't breathe. She stooped to get close to Jack's face. He kissed her gently. She sighed. He kissed her again, his lips with a touch more pressure on them. A feeling of warmth engulfed her, and she placed her hands on his shoulders. Jack sensed her signal of acceptance, stood and encircled her waist with his good arm. His lips caressed and moved on hers until she stopped thinking. Feelings of warmth, of happiness, and of an emotion or desire she couldn't name filled her senses when his body pressed on hers. Her body tingled as he touched her, and his body was hard and strong. Her arms reached up to touch his hair with her hands, sliding the strands through her fingers. Her senses filled with his kiss, his touch… He ended the kiss. She couldn't face him.

Jack sat. "So when can you take me to the saloon?"

Still in a daze, Lina couldn't understand his question. "Saloon?'

He took her hand and kissed her palm. "Yeah."

Praise for L. M. Gonzalez

Dedication

To my son, Albert Daniel Gonzalez—
he is my inspiration and sounding board.
To the authors in this wonderful, magical,
and rowdy Wylder West series.
To my editor, Nan Swanson,
who makes my stories so much better.

Chapter 1

"I found one, Miss Lina. A sunflower." Five-year-old Hortencia held up a dried stem she'd uprooted.

Evangelina Gaitan laughed. "You may be right, Hortencia. Let's keep walking, so we can stay warm."

She led her young students through the field of dead grass and melting mounds of snow. Late February in Wylder, Wyoming could still be icy cold, and snow could fall at any time. The voices of the children were squeaky, and a squeal erupted every now and then. Older voices of the teenagers, Alejandro and Rafael, tried to sound more grownup. Alejandro was thirteen and a loner. Rafael, a muscular young man who rarely talked, was a fourteen-year-old orphan who acted as their messenger and would pick up mail at the post office.

Lina had given the children a list of wildflowers they'd be able to pick once spring arrived. The unrelenting snow for the past few weeks had kept the children inside and misbehaving more than usual. They needed to be outside in the crisp fresh air for a few minutes.

Sister Cecilia, the Mother Superior, frowned upon frivolousness, especially as Ash Wednesday and the Lenten season were next week. However, children needed a respite from prayer and silence. Lina sighed. God knew she'd needed fun while growing up in the St. Thomas Catholic church orphanage, her permanent

1

home. She'd been twelve years old when she and her family had traveled from Texas to Wylder, Wyoming. Her parents had died in a wagon accident just outside of town.

A couple of little girls ran up and told her there were no flowers. The boys wanted to climb the trees and refused to play the flower game. Funny, they started so small to eschew anything that smacked of a little romance. Lina breathed in the chilly morning air. A shiver ran through her. However, she liked the beginning of a new day—many possibilities. In her darkest moments, the darkest of nights, the mornings would always bring hope.

"Miss Lina, there's only dead weeds out here," Salvador, a ten-year-old mischievous imp, said in Spanish. "Can't I climb a tree instead? Flowers are for girls."

Lina grinned. "First of all, speak English. The more you practice, the better you'll get. Second of all, I'm glad you know girls like flowers. That's why you need to know what kinds there are."

He kicked at a small stone and stared at the ground. His curly black hair was clean now. She remembered when he'd first arrived—dirty, malnourished, and scared.

"Go on, go climb a tree." The boy ran off before Lina finished speaking. "Be careful."

"I will, Miss Lina."

Lina laughed, gazing at the surroundings, and still keeping an eye on the eight children she had under her supervision. She grabbed two little girls' hands. "Let's keep walking and talk about wildflowers."

The field, a small flat piece of ground that flourished

with wildflowers and waving grasses in the spring, extended for half a mile behind the Catholic Church. Lina lifted her head and breathed in the crisp, cold air. She loved being outside, but the children should return to the school. Before she could call them to line up, she heard her name.

Alejandro ran to her, screaming, "Miss Lina, Miss Lina!" Rafael and Salvador accompanied him. "We found a dead man!"

Lina's heart jolted. "What?" A feeling of dread filled her. A dead man? Who? Why? Behind the church?

Alejandro grabbed her hand. "Come on, Miss Lina." He ran toward a tree in the far corner of the field.

"No, wait," she called. "Maybe we should get the sheriff. He's the one who should take care of this. We have no business getting involved."

The other two boys ran ahead.

"Boys, come back! It's dangerous. The killer could still be nearby." She shouted, but they kept moving. She had no choice but to follow.

When she reached the spot with Alejandro, he said, "Look." He pointed to a tree at the end of the property that belonged to the church.

Lina saw a man lying face down, sprawled among the crushed weeds. He wore a long black coat and long tall boots, and his black hat lay on the ground next to him.

"There's another one over there," Alejandro said.

"Another one?" Lina gasped. What on earth? *"Dios mio."* She exclaimed to God in Spanish, forgetting her rule.

Her body shook as she walked to the other man a few feet away. This man—actually a boy—was face up.

His smooth face with closed eyes seemed as if he were asleep. His dark hair waved in the breeze. He was also dressed in black but wore a short coat.

Lina's heart beat faster. "We—we—have to alert the sheriff. We—we—must—What do we do?" Lina squared her shoulders. She had to take charge as the teacher, the adult.

"Come on, boys. Let's go back to the school. Rafael, go to the sheriff with a message." The boy nodded and ran to do her bidding.

She hustled Salvador and the other boys away by grabbing hands and giving them a gentle pull away from the dead men.

A groan sounded—from the man in the long coat. He was alive. Lina wanted to keep walking. The long years of teaching she'd received from Father Bellamy and the nuns stopped her. *God calls on us to help others.* She turned back and neared the man. No more sounds emitted from his mouth. She turned to leave. Another groan. The children surrounded her.

"Children, go back to the school. Alejandro, lead them back," she said.

"Yes, ma'am," he said.

"Tell Father Pete what is happening."

Lina inched toward the man and bent down. She touched his black hair. At the softness of it, she snaked her hand back. He moved his head on the ground. His face was muddied, and hair was matted to his cheek.

"Help…me…" His voice sounded scratchy, and his body was now trembling. Was he cold? How long had he been lying here? "My brother… Where…?"

"He's a few feet away. I don't think he's—I mean…" She stopped because she didn't know how to

4

tell him.

Lina shot to her feet. "Alejandro! Alejandro, tell Father Pete to come here and bring the cart. The man is alive!"

She turned to the man. "Father Pete is on his way to help you. Stay still. You might have broken bones," she said.

He was tall, broad-shouldered, and as dirty and unkempt as Salvador had been—not malnourished, however. Lina moved away. She'd never been that close to a man before, not since her father. Her heart jumped. Her body still shook with reaction.

"They wanted—to-to-to—kill me," he said. His voice was hoarse, but a little stronger now. He moved to sit up, but moaned and fell backward. "I'm cold—Check my—little—brother. Is-is he-he all right?"

"I'm sorry. I'm not sure," she said.

"Dammit. I'm go-go-ing to-to kill those… Shit." He trembled, but grabbed his left shoulder.

He had such big hands. She looked at hers, which would fit in one of his and disappear. "Please lie still. Father Pete will be here soon."

"Are-are-are you a-a-a nun?" The man's teeth chattered. "An-an-an angel?"

"No, I'm not a nun or an angel," she said.

He smiled. "Thank God. Not-not-not ready to-to die-die yet."

"Lina, what is happening?" Father Pete asked.

Lina heaved a sigh. "*Ay,* Father Pete. The children found this man. He's hurt and cold. And there's another one, younger, but I think—he's dead." She whispered the last word.

The man heard . "Dead? My little-little-little bro-

bro-brother…?"

"Stay still, *muchacho*," the priest said. "Alejandro will arrive soon with the cart, and we'll take you to the school and to a room to tend to you. I'll take care of your brother as well. May I know your name—and his?"

The man closed his eyes, sighed, and then opened them. "Joa-quin-Jack-Jack-Pa-pa-pa-lermo. Bro-brother —Jimmy…" The man's hoarse voice broke.

"I'm sorry, *hijo*. He is in heaven now. At peace," the priest said.

"Peace, Fa-Fa-Father—? Not me. Kill those bastards…" Jack hissed and passed out.

Lina's body trembled.

****

Jack heard voices around him, but couldn't make them out. Where was he? Warmth filled him. He'd been so damn cold. Where was Jimmy? A priest had said he was in heaven. *Yeah, Jimmy would be.* He wouldn't, though. He'd been in hell most of his life. Why would he go to heaven when he died? That bastard, Falwell, he'd have to die and go to hell, too.

A beautiful woman in white had sat next to him—a dream? She wore a mantilla. He'd glimpsed a few black curls fringing the edge. If she wasn't an angel, then she was a nun. Every woman he met was either a nun or a whore. Women in between didn't pay him any mind. Especially in this town of Wylder, Wyoming. Only women from the East traveled to this dusty town, most searching for a husband. And he would never be husband material. His poor excuse of a father had shown him how well suited he would be to be a husband and father.

Excruciating pain. What the hell? Needles were being stuck into his shoulder.

"Ayyyyyy." Who screamed? He never showed anyone how much he ached—either in his heart or his hide. He wasn't sure he had a heart anymore—with Jimmy dead. Pain of another kind sent his body trembling. Another scream, a primal yell of pain, yearning, and a violent desire for revenge swirled in his brain.

He opened his eyes and the beautiful woman sat in a chair near his bed. Her eyes gazed at him, but her body was poised for flight. Why was she scared? He couldn't move. His whole body ached. He tried to lift his hand and couldn't.

"Weak… Why?" His throat hurt. "Water."

The woman jumped to her feet. Lifting his head with her hand, she held a cup of water to his mouth. He drank greedily, but she held the cup away after a few sips.

"Slow down," she said.

"Where am I?"

"In a room in the school, the St, Thomas Catholic School and orphanage," she said. "You've been here for three days. The doctor came, took out the bullet, and you had a terrible fever, but—I think—you're better now. Are you?"

Three days. Falwell and his outfit would be long gone now. He struggled to get up, but again his weakness and a firm hand on his chest held him down. "Don't move. You have a terrible wound. Are you hungry?"

"No, maybe later." He stared at her—her dress was more gray than white, and she still wore the mantilla."

"Don't you ever take that thing off?"

At her puzzled look, he said, "The mantilla. I'd like to see the face of the woman who saved my life." He gave her a crooked smile.

"I didn't save your life. Father Pete, the children, and the doctor did," she said.

He sighed. "Ummm… What's your name?"

"Evangelina Gaitan," she said.

"Evangelina. Pretty name. Means good news," he said. "You were probably born on April eighth."

She gasped. "How—did—did you know?"

"Before I—I— My mother was a saint—and she knew a lot about saints." He tried to smile, but remembered his mother constantly knocked down by his father, who would leave her hurt and bleeding. "Yeah, she knew a lot of saints. Too bad—bad—she didn't marry one."

Before he slept again, he heard her whisper, "And your birthday is on July twenty-sixth, for St. Joachim, Jesus' grandfather."

When Jack woke again, he was alone. He wondered where the pretty Evangelina had gone. He didn't feel as weak. At least he could lift his hands and move his feet without feeling as though he pushed against a mountain. An ache pierced his heart when he remembered Jimmy. He would never hear him sing again. If Falwell walked to the edge of hell, Jack would follow him.

Jimmy's death would be avenged—by him. He'd had no choice but to take the boy with him when he joined the Falwell gang. Jimmy had been his responsibility ever since they'd run away from home. He'd been thirteen and Jimmy five. They'd lived on the streets for two years before a woman, Mrs. Myra Hildebrand, had taken them in. She'd fed them, sent them to school, and read to them from the books in her library. They'd lived with her until she died, three years later.

Then he and Jimmy were back on the streets until Jack met Falwell. Jack had stayed with the gang for fourteen years. At the end of that time, Falwell had seen fit to kill him. Pure greed. The bastard hadn't wanted to share the loot they'd gotten at the bank in Cheyenne. He'd killed the Palermo brothers, or tried to.

Jack also had a beef with Rufus, a member of the gang. The man had left him for dead. He'd exact revenge on the Irishman as soon as he took care of Falwell.

A woman entered with a tray. "Here's your supper. You haven't eaten in three days. You must build up your strength."

This stocky and robust woman had a round face wreathed in smiles, no hesitancy about her. "I'm Sister Anne. Come now. Sit up. You can't eat lying down." She adjusted the pillows and helped him sit up.

"Where's the other girl? Nun?"

"Oh, Lina? She's not a nun, though she wanted to be. Mother Superior didn't think she had the calling. Lina needs to find a man to marry and have babies. That's where her calling is."

Jack became pensive for a minute. *Marry and have babies.* Another woman had entered his life, totally unsuitable. *Ah, hell.* He wasn't looking for a woman. He wanted Falwell to pay.

Sister Anne didn't stick around. This woman was all business and duty. Jack began to eat—pinto beans and rice. And tortillas—soft, and their floury smell took him back to his mom's kitchen before his dad's invasion. Where was Lina? Not that he could give in to temptation except to look at her and talk to her. Just the same, he wanted to see her again.

****

Lina knelt on the floor in her plain room with only a small bed and a chest of drawers for her clothes. She'd covered her bed with a colorful quilt her mother had made.

She'd returned from the chapel after morning prayers. Mother Superior hadn't believed she was meant to take orders, but Lina would join the nuns for their daily prayers. Now, she would reflect and pray for an hour before she would go to morning mass, then help Sister Anne make breakfast, all accomplished before seven in the morning. Her classes began at eight. Her schedule was full from morning to night, but Lina didn't mind. She wanted to be useful. The orphanage had been her home for so long, and she wanted to repay them for taking care of her.

Now, however, her thoughts were full of the man she'd helped rescue—Jack Palermo. Father Pete and the nuns hadn't allowed her, an unmarried girl, to tend to the man. However, she'd sat with him yesterday afternoon, after her class, until Sister Anne had taken in his supper. Everyone else had been busy tending to the duties of the orphanage and the church.

Lina squared her shoulders and emptied her mind, reflecting on holiness and prayer. She recited the prayers of the rosary she held in her hands. Her mind wavered, and she saw Jack—his black hair touching the pillow, closed eyes, his long eyelashes. She longed to touch his face and his chest, bare except where it was covered by the bandage on his shoulder. Her eyes followed the length of his body down to his uncovered feet. The blanket was too short to cover all of him. She couldn't see him under the blanket, but—

"*Ay, Dios mi.* Forgive me. I'll concentrate," Lina

whispered. The sight of Jack had caused her body heat to rise, her hands to shake, and her heartbeat to speed up. Feelings of restlessness had assailed her lately. Her duties were not enough. She fingered the rosary beads and continued praying. In spite of several forays into sinful thoughts, she managed to finish. She stood, placed her rosary on the bedside table, and left the room.

The kitchen was warm and cozy, the best heated room in the orphanage.

"Ah, Lina," said Sister Anne. Forty years of age, she stood stocky and red-cheeked at the work table. "Come scramble the eggs. I have the biscuits in the oven. I also made oatmeal. No bacon this morning. Salvador went to the mercantile, but the ranch hadn't delivered yet. A blessing, if you ask me. It's the end of the month, and we don't have money until next month."

Lina took a deep breath before she walked to the table and began cracking eggs into a bowl. She willed herself not to feel this urgency to go to Jack's bedside. Her body burned to be next to him. She made the sign of the cross.

"Are you feeling sick, Lina?" Sister Anne's brow wrinkled in concern.

"No, Sister. I'm fine," she said. She poured the eggs into the pan and stirred.

Once finished cooking, Lina sat at a long table in the large dining room to eat and looked forward to her morning class.

"This afternoon I'm going to help Mother Superior with the end-of-the-month paperwork to mail to the diocese. You will have to check on the wounded man, Lina. Make sure he's feeling well. Maybe you can read from the Bible to him."

Lina's heart swelled in anticipation, but she remained still. "Yes, Sister."

During class, Lina had her students find pictures of flowers in books, draw them, and write the correct name under each flower, in both English and Spanish. She helped her students when they needed her assistance. Her mind, however, wandered with thoughts of Jack.

Finally, she was outside his door. She knocked. Would he be awake? She entered the room. Jack reclined on the bed. He had his eyes closed and his hands crossed on his chest.

"You returned. The angel." He grinned.

Her heart jumped. "I'm not an angel—Mr. Palermo."

"You sure looked like one to me out in the field where I'd been left for dead." His smile disappeared, and his face contorted in anger. "What happened to my brother?"

"Father Pete held a funeral mass and the undertaker buried him in the church graveyard," she said.

"Thank you."

"I'm—I'm—sorry." She hated to be hesitant, but he frightened her, not only because he was a man, but because he could get so angry. The people she lived with seldom showed anger.

"Why? You didn't kill him." His angry expression became more pronounced. He moved his legs. "I want to get out of this bed. I don't need to be babied."

"You have—to stay—in bed. The doctor said. At least—for at least two weeks." Lina still stood.

"I have things to do. I can't lie around in bed all day. Get that doctor over here," Jack said. "I'll tell him how I really feel."

Doc Sullivan stood in the doorway. "I'll tell you what you need to do, Jack. And that's stay in bed. If you intend to get on a horse, which I'm assuming you do, you'll break open your wound and bleed to death before you can accomplish whatever is so damned urgent."

Jack glared at the doctor.

"Good afternoon, Lina." Doc Sullivan bowed to Lina.

"Good afternoon," she said in a soft voice. From the time she'd met him, Lina thought the doctor was a very handsome man with his dark hair and green eyes. But he was now married to a very pretty woman, Miss Eliza Jane O'Hanlon. Well, she used to be a miss. Now she was a *senora*.

The doctor examined the wound and changed the bandage. "No infection, and healing well. Mind the nice nuns here, Jack. Two more weeks, then you can go your way." He packed up his supplies and left.

Lina walked with the doctor to the door, then returned to sit on the chair by Jack's bedside.

"Don't you have nunly duties to do?" he sneered.

He didn't like her. Actually, he didn't seem to like anyone. His spirit was broken—as was his heart after his little brother's death. What kind of a life had he led to become such an angry man?

"I can read—to you," she said.

"I'm not a child you have to amuse, darling." He closed his eyes.

"If you're sleepy, I can—leave. I don't—want to—bother you—while you rest." She stood. She took her rosary from her dress pocket and with the cross she blessed him.

"Don't waste your prayers on me," he said.

"Prayers—are never—wasted, Mr. Palermo," she said.

"Yeah, well. That's what you think. My mother prayed and prayed—Shit. Let me sleep, will you?" He closed his eyes again. This time he also turned his face toward the wall.

Lina's stomach flipped. Her eyes threatened to fill with tears. She didn't understand her reactions. This man held no significance in her life except as another human being who needed her help.

"Yes. Another of the nuns will check on you later." She walked away and glanced back one more time before she opened the door and left.

Chapter 2

Jack opened his eyes and regretted sending Lina away. He'd wanted to see her all morning. Part of his restlessness was because the hours had gone by and he hadn't seen her. Other nuns had been in to check on him and bring in his meals. But Lina hadn't visited him. When she had, he'd been rude to her. He had to leave. No matter what the doc said. The more time he spent in bed, the more time Falwell had to get away. He also had to visit Jimmy's gravesite and bid him goodbye. His heart contracted with pain. He'd vowed to protect him and he'd let his little brother down. He'd only lived twenty-two years, but he'd given Jack a reason to live. Now, he had no reason to play it safe. He would kill Falwell, and then he didn't give a damn what happened to him. He had nothing to live for anymore.

His thoughts returned to Lina. No, the woman was virginal, practically a nun. She'd never survive the kind of life he could give her. Besides, she was probably as thin as a rail under her sisterly gray garb. The attire didn't allow any curves to show, if she had any. He liked his women full-figured and busty. Past time he paid a visit to one of the ladies of the Wylder County Social Club. He smiled at the thought of Miss Addie. She was the kind of woman he'd want to meet—tough and took no nonsense, the kind of woman he'd wished his mother could have been. Maybe she had been once, but his bastard of a father had killed any spark of life in her along with the decency of her life.

As usual, when Jack remembered his father, anger filled him, and every vein in his body pulsed with the desire to kill. News had reached them a few years back that the man had died. Jack couldn't rest until he was sure. Because if he wasn't, he'd kill him, too.

A knock sounded on his door. Lina had returned! His heart lifted, and he squelched his angry thoughts. He hadn't liked bringing fear into her eyes. He didn't want to be like his father and scare defenseless women. But Sister Anne entered his room, not Lina.

"Now, you listen to me, young man. Doc Sullivan told me to keep an eagle eye on you because you have a mind to leave us." The nun, who should have been angelic, or at least kindly, shook her fist at him as she admonished him. "I'll not have you leave my establishment the worse for wear. You will stay in that bed if I have to hog-tie you to it. Do you understand?"

"Yes," he said.

"Yes?" She lifted an eyebrow.

"Yes, Sister Anne," he said.

She crossed her arms on her ample bosom. "I can see you need a firm hand. Lina is too kind. She sees good in everyone as I'm sure she sees it in you. And while I tend to believe there has to be good in everyone, as we all are God's children, I know from my many years on this earth some people need more of a push to be good than others. And you're one of those, Mr. Palermo."

Jack nodded and remained silent. This woman was scary.

"I will send Sister Beatrice to tend to you. Lina has her schoolroom duties and doesn't need to be in here with you." Sister Anne twitched the blanket up his chest, baring more of his feet and legs.

"Do you think you can bring me another blanket?" Jack asked. "This one doesn't cover me. I'll catch a chill and have to be with you for a longer time." He grinned.

Sister Anne glared, and then she guffawed. "You are a sly one. A charmer, too, aren't you? Well, you can't charm me, young man. Some of the best have tried. But you have a point. I'll get you a blanket."

The nun trotted to the door. "Well?"

"Thank you, Sister Anne." He winked at her.

"Shameful man," she said. "You should say ten Our Fathers and ten Hail Marys."

Funny how he could remember the prayers as soon as the nun said the names. But he hadn't prayed in years.

Another knock and Lina peered in. She walked slowly to the bed.

"I came—to tell you—Sister Beatrice—will be the one checking—on you from now on. I hope—you get—better soon."

"Have you ever had a *novio*, Lina?"

"A boyfriend? No, never. Young ladies don't have boyfriends. They get betrothed with their father's permission. No, a *novio* would never be permitted," Lina said.

"Just what I thought." He grinned. "I prefer women who are more experienced."

"Experienced in what? I can—cook and bake. And sew." The smile she gave him lighted up her face. His heart gave an unwanted leap.

She was naïve. He didn't have the heart to tell her the hard truths of life. He gave her a small smile. "Yeah, that's what I mean."

"I have to go. Get—well soon." She pulled out her rosary and blessed him again. This time he closed his eyes as she waved the cross over him. Calmness filled him for a second, like it had the time he sat by a river and taught Jimmy how to fish. However, when he opened his eyes, Lina was gone and so was the sense of peace.

****

Lina sat behind her desk in the schoolroom where she taught her classes. The room was small and plain, with a wooden floor and small crude tables and chairs for the children. A blackboard covered half of the front wall. Lina's small desk and chair sat in front of the blackboard. To the right side of her desk stood a little shelf filled with children's books and readers. At the back of the room, wooden shelves had been built for the children to store their school supplies.

Today was Ash Wednesday, the first day of Lent, a time of fasting and abstinence from eating meat. Lina sighed. Abstaining from eating meat wasn't a problem. The orphanage seldom had any to offer. The diet was mostly beans, rice, and potatoes. In the summer and fall, their little vegetable garden yielded fresh tomatoes, green bell peppers, carrots, and peas. So the kitchen at the orphanage had a good supply of canned vegetables through the winter, also.

Lina had finished teaching the children about the day and now, on her request, they were writing down what they planned to do for the Lenten season until Easter, forty days away. She'd emphasized they didn't have to give up eating their favorite food or drink. The emphasis centered on achieving a purpose that would make them better people.

Hortencia raised her hand.

18

"What's your question?"

"If I stop hitting my friend Roberto, would that be good?"

Lina smiled. "Yes, Hortencia."

The little girl angered easily, and Roberto loved to tease her.

"Okay." Lina picked up her pencil and, holding it very tightly, began to write.

If I stop having these sinful thoughts about Jack, would that be good?

Her heart jumped. Why couldn't she stop thinking about him? She'd never experienced these feelings for any other man. Not that a lot of men other than priests had regularly crossed her path—there was the doctor, who visited the orphanage when he was needed. However, most of the time the nuns had home remedies they used to treat themselves and the children. When she went to town for supplies, she would see men, a lot of them very rough-looking. She would see the sheriff, and Finn Wylder at the mercantile. None of these men sparked an interest in her. Why Jack, of all men?

The bell signaling lunch startled Lina out of her reverie. The noise and bustle of the children resounded as they put their supplies in the cupboards on the wall and lined up to walk to the dining room.

They left amid chatter of whether or not they could eat meat, and other voices shouting they only had potatoes to eat. Lina followed, but planned to eat only a small serving, her one meal of the day.

Sister Anne bustled in. "Lina, I need you. Sister Beatrice has to go with Father Pete to a church member's house—she can't tend to Jack's wound. You'll have to do it."

Lina trembled, and her stomach flip-flopped. "But—Sister Anne, I've only changed the bandage once. What if—I hurt him?"

"I barely finished with lunch. The others will have to do cleanup since I'm still helping the Mother Superior with the bookkeeping. Come along. You can eat later."

The nun pulled Lina along. On the way, they stopped by the hall cupboard to get the supplies needed to do the care of the wound.

"Water is already heating on the stove," Sister Anne said and bustled away.

Lina walked to the kitchen and poured the hot water into a small bucket, then hurried to Jack's room. Since her hands were full, she didn't knock but pushed the door in.

Jack sat on the edge of the bed trying to stand.

"What are you doing?" Lina rushed in and quickly placed the bucket and linens on a small table near the bed as she confronted him. "You can't get up. You'll pop open your stitches!"

"I have to get the hell out of here." Jack inhaled. "Dammit! I can't be this weak. I have to go. Have to find Falwell."

With her heart beating overtime, Lina ventured to say, "Revenge is hardly a good reason to re-injure yourself. Please lie down again."

"Will you lie down with me?" He grinned.

"I—I can't—we're not—not married…" Lina didn't know what to say or where to look.

Jack laughed. "You said you weren't going to tend to me anymore."

"The other nuns are busy. Your bandage needs to be changed and your wound cleaned."

He huffed.

Carefully, trying not to lean too much on him since the wound was on his left shoulder, Lina took the old bandage off, untying the knot and cutting it away with scissors where it stuck. She took linen, wet it in the hot water, and wrung it of excess water as much as she could by folding it and pushing at it with a pair of scissors.

"This will be hot, but I need to clean the wound," she said.

To his credit, Jack didn't flinch. Lina was a bit clumsy, both because she had done this only once before and also because of his nearness, though he kept his eyes closed. His warm skin was hard and smooth. She'd never touched any part of a man's body before, or anybody's, really. An orphanage wasn't conducive to affection, though Lina tried to be as caring to the children as she could.

"I'm finished. Thank you for—being patient with me." Lina grabbed the soiled bandage and threw it into a pail under the bed. "Is there anything else you need?"

"What kind of fragrance do you use?"

"Fragrance?" Lina wondered what he meant. She always carried a sachet of wildflowers in her pocket, but those were from last spring. Surely, they had no scent anymore.

"You smell like a garden." Jack held her hand and caressed her fingers. He pulled her down.

She'd never been this close to a man. She gasped. "I—I probably smell like eggs and tortillas. I—helped to—cook breakfast this morning."

Jack pulled her still closer. He nuzzled her neck. "No, not breakfast. A garden."

She glanced at his lips, full and straight. She'd never

noticed a man's mouth before. Was he going to kiss her? Her heart thudded fast. Surely, he could hear it.

A loud noise made him loosen his hold. She stood and grabbed the pail of soiled linens, the bucket, and the scissors.

"I have to go, Mr. Palermo. One of the nuns will check on you later."

Lina tried not to run as she left the room.

****

Jack tried to move in the bed, but the pain prevented him. Falwell journeyed farther away from him. The man needed to pay for what he'd done—for leaving him for dead, but mainly for killing his little brother.

Maybe he should agree to have Lina read to him. Did the place have other reading material besides the Bible? Maybe they had a newspaper. Perhaps he could find out if someone had spotted the Falwells. No, the bastard was too smart to be seen and reported on. His brother, Houston "Jugbutt" Jenkins, was as dumb as an ox, though. If anyone would sabotage Falwell's plans, his brother would be the one to do it. Jack counted on him making a grave mistake.

Jack tried to sit up. Lying flat on his back made him irritable. He tried to inch up to the pillow, but he only succeeded in wrenching his injured shoulder, which made him cry out in pain. Thankfully, no one heard him be such a weakling. Weakness wasn't tolerated in a Palermo. His father had beaten that wisdom into Jack's head countless times as a boy.

The admission was hard for Jack, but he'd been a crybaby once. Every setback made him weep, and his mother would always hold him in her arms, soothe his ruffled feathers, and kiss him on his cheek. Until the day his father arrived home, from whatever temporary job he'd gotten to put liquor in his belly, and seen him in his mother's arms. Both of them received a beating that day that Jack never forgot. He didn't remember where two-year-old Jimmy had been. Jack hadn't been able to open his battered eyes for days. Later, Jimmy told him he'd hidden under the bed until Jack had begun to heal. From that day forward, Jack hadn't cried another tear. He'd been ten years old.

Weakness had no place in a man's life. That's why he battled this banishment to a bed. He'd be fine if he could only escape, if he could sit up. *Dammit.* He couldn't, not without help.

Father Pete Orozco entered his room. "Good morning, my son."

Jack cringed at the term "son." To him, neither the word nor the sentiment had any good meaning.

"How are you this morning? Have you had breakfast?" The man smiled, holding his Bible tightly to his heart.

"Yeah—I mean, yes, Father, thank you," Jack said.

"I wondered if you'd like to speak to me, maybe make your confession," the priest said.

"I don't think so." Jack flipped the blanket. "You could help me sit up. I can't on my own."

"Of course." Father Pete placed his Bible carefully on the table beside Jack's bed.

For a wiry man, he was strong. He grabbed Jack around the shoulders and the waist and had him half-reclined with little effort.

"Thanks," Jack said. He settled the blankets to cover his body.

"Now." The priest pushed his spectacles up his nose.

"Will you begin?"

"Begin what?" Jack's irritation grew by the minute. Wound or no wound, if this pushy priest didn't leave in the next two minutes, Jack would find an object to throw at him and knock him out cold.

"Your confession, of course," the man said.

"I'm not confessing, Father. I doubt I'm Catholic anymore. I haven't darkened a church since I was ten."

"You were baptized a Catholic. You're a Catholic until death." The priest said the words as a declaration address.

"I don't have anything to confess. Talk to me in three weeks. Then, maybe I'll confess that I've avenged my little brother's death."

Father Pete's stoic demeanor faded a little. "Do you mean to say that you're planning to commit murder? That's a grave sin."

"Grave is right, Father. And not murder one person. Murder two men. And both of them will have very grave endings." Jack frowned at the priest, then smirked. "Priests take a seal of the confessional, don't they?"

Father Pete slowly nodded.

Jack grinned. "You can't tell anyone what I told you, can you?"

Father Pete's face went gray for a few seconds. Then he picked up his Bible and held it close to his heart again. His face composed, and his features changed to those of compassion. "You have a lot of anger, my son. When you're ready, come to me and confide in me. I can help you, with God on our side. Anger and thoughts of revenge only take us away from God—and away from every good thing there is in this life. You could be happy. Find a wife. Have a family. You're a very young man."

"So are you, Father Pete. Why did you take up priestly orders when you could find yourself a good woman?" Jack didn't like himself at the moment, arguing and putting down a priest. He could see his mother's face, ashamed of him and embarrassed.

"I did—once. I believed I had found happiness. She was the most beautiful woman I'd ever met, and I fell in love with her the moment I saw her. My wedding day was one day away.

"What happened?" Jack was interested in spite of himself—a result of the boredom of lying in bed, probably.

"She'd fallen in love with my name, my house, and my money...or rather my father's money. When my father lost both his money and the house—and practically his name—on a turn of a card in a poker game, she left me. She said she wasn't about to marry a homely man with no money or position. I was so angry I wanted to kill her." Father Pete hugged the Bible closer to his chest.

"Our priest, Father Shane, who'd been visiting with my father, brought me to my senses. My father had too much at stake to risk a hint of scandal, so Father Shane sent me here, out west, to Father Bellamy. My father didn't care where. I've been here ever since."

Jack stared at Father Pete, believing him. Through the years, there wasn't much Jack hadn't seen or heard.

"Everyone here in this town of Wylder has a story, Jack. We try to learn a new way to deal with our pasts instead of continuing on the same destructive path. I hope you find yours, too. I'll be here when you're ready."

Father Pete left Jack in a daze. His ears buzzed with

the priest's story, and he remembered scenes from his past, the brutality of his father, but also the love and warmth from his mother and Jimmy.

He remembered a quote he'd never forgotten: *No one goes west for the scenery.*

Chapter 3

Lina decided to take three children to visit Jack, to make his day more bearable. He preferred staying alone in his room. She hoped, for the sake of the children, he would at least listen. In spite of objections from both the Mother Superior and Sister Anne, Lina was teaching the children to see the Lenten season as a time of not only sacrifice but also hope. She instructed her students to write a paragraph on their goals for Easter.

Salvador and Hortencia had an idea to put on a little play. They wanted to rehearse in front of someone before presenting it to Father Pete, the nuns, and the other children.

One afternoon, after class ended, Lina led them from the schoolroom down the hallway to Jack's room.

"Wait here. Let me tell him what we're going to do, so he'll be prepared."

Jack didn't move when she entered. He had his face turned toward the wall.

"Mr. Palermo?" Lina wished she weren't tentative. She cleared her throat. "I have a surprise for you."

Slowly, he turned to face her with a scowl. "I don't like surprises."

"Do you feel well? Have you eaten?"

"Yeah," he said.

"I—I know—how hard it must be for you..."

He pulled the blankets up to cover himself with a

quick movement. "You don't know a damn thing."

Lina swallowed, her heart in her throat. "I suppose I don't. But—I know how it feels to be sick—and not be able to do—what you want. I was very sick with fever when I first came to the orphanage after my parents were killed in a wagon accident. Father Bellamy was here at the time. He took care of me until I got well."

Jack didn't show any emotion or say a single word.

"He made my days better by reading to me and acting out scenes from the books for me. He made me laugh. I was happy for a few minutes out of my day. Three children want to put on a little play for you. Call it—a rehearsal. Their presentation is this evening after supper. Will you let them—practice for you?"

Jack turned his face away from her. He took a deep breath as she watched his nearly bare chest, trying not to wonder what the rest of him looked like.

"All right," he finally said.

"They're little, and they haven't had many happy moments in their lives either. Please be kind to them." Lina smiled and went to the door to let the children in.

She heard Jack mutter, "I don't know how to be kind."

Salvador and Hortencia ran in and immediately started telling Jack about their play. Alejandro, more hesitant, entered the room slowly. Standing in front of people made him nervous.

"Are you comfortable, Mr. Palermo? Do you want me to help you sit up a little?"

"Yeah," Jack said. "I hate lying around helpless."

"I'm sorry." Lina put her arm around him and let him lean on her as he leveraged himself up. Without a word, Alejandro moved to the other side of the bed, moving it a few inches from the wall, and helped Jack and Lina.

"Thanks," Jack said.

Lina smiled. "The play is short. We won't be here all afternoon. Don't worry." She motioned to the children. "Begin."

The play was brief, five minutes. The children talked about the meaning of Lent, what they'd decided to work on for the season, and then said they'd composed a song of hope. Alejandro picked up his guitar he'd leaned against the wall and began playing. The children sang. Alejandro, who had the strongest and most musical voice, joined in. Lina wanted him to sing in the church choir, but he refused.

Lina's eyes filled with tears. She clapped when they were finished, proud of her students, and she told them so, then added, "Now, go back to the room. I'll be there soon."

"Bye, Mr. Palermo," Hortencia said. She stood on tiptoes and kissed him on the cheek. "Don't cry. God loves you."

"Bye, Miss Lina." Hortencia skipped out of the room. Salvador also bade her farewell. Alejandro smiled at her before he walked out.

"Mr. Palermo?" Lina eyed him, feeling concerned. His eyes did appear teary.

"I'm fine." He slid down the pillows to lie prone. "I'd like to rest now."

"Thank you for listening to the children."

Before she opened the door, Jack said, "My little brother sang. We called him 'Jimmy the Songbird.' I'll never hear him sing again."

"I'm sorry."

"Yeah."

Lina's heart ached for him. She knew the pain of loss and loneliness, hoping for someone to love, someone who loved her, and finding no one. Duty and responsibility ruled. For Jack, he had revenge on his mind. She wished—and prayed—he would change his mind and try another way to live his life without his little brother. He was on a dangerous path. He could be killed as well. Lina knew the thought of being killed himself didn't bother Jack in the least.

****

Two weeks later, Doc Sullivan returned to the orphanage and gave Jack permission to leave his bed, but he cautioned him to move slowly and keep the sling on.

Sister Anne had been in the room with him, and as she saw Doc out the door, she promised him Jack would follow instructions.

"How are you going to make sure, Sister Anne? I'm leaving right now," Jack said and stood, or tried to. His legs buckled, and he floundered back onto the bed. "What the hell?"

"You mind your tongue, young man." Sister Anne had the audacity to grin. "You've been in bed for three weeks. You're going to feel dizzy the first few times you stand. Take it slow, like Doc said."

"How much longer will this take?" Exasperation filled him. The sparse room was closing in on him. Time was running out.

"Not long. You're strong. You haven't eaten. Good food will strengthen you even more. I'll send Sister Beatrice in with breakfast. Get up for short spurts. Get your sea legs back."

"Sea legs? I've never been on a boat," Jack said.

"Figure of speech, young man." Sister Anne bustled away.

Before his breakfast arrived, Jack managed to climb back on the bed in a half-reclining position. He hit the blanket. Frustration built up at his helplessness. He blamed Falwell for this. The man ran free. Jimmy was six feet under. Rage filled Jack near to bursting. He couldn't stand much more of this weakness. Men weren't supposed to be weak.

His father's contorted, enraged face blurred the colorless wall Jack stared at.

You're a weakling, boy. A fist to the face. *Don't ever let me see you in your mother's arms again.* Pain blinded him as another blow struck his left eye. *Be a man,* cabrón, *not a* vieja. Jack finally passed out.

Pounding on the door caused Jack to open his eyes. He'd been unaware he'd closed them.

Sister Beatrice entered the room with a broad grin on her face and a cheery greeting. She carried his breakfast of eggs, sausage, and tortillas on a metal tray. The nun placed a cup on the tray and poured coffee.

"I'll return in a few minutes and pour you more coffee," she said.

Jack eyed the breakfast. The smell of the food reached his nose but didn't make him hungry. After his mother died from one too many beatings, Jack had run and taken Jimmy with him. He wasn't going to remain and watch his little brother die. Jack moaned. He'd lost him anyway through his own damned fault. If anyone had to die, he should have been the one. Jimmy was goodness, full of song and light. Jack was hard, filled with darkness, filled with vengeful fury. Unbidden, Jack remembered Father Pete's words.

Anger and thoughts of revenge only take us away from God—and away from every good thing there is in this life.

Jack placed his tray on the table by the bed. He sipped the hot coffee, better than any he'd drunk on the run. He took a deep breath, and the pain in his shoulder ripped through him. *Dammit.* He finished the coffee and exchanged the cup for the tray. Food would strengthen him. All right, he'd eat.

Happy Beatrice returned to refill his coffee and take the tray.

Jack pushed himself off the bed again. His legs held him up a little longer. Dizziness still overwhelmed, and he sat. Thankfully, the pain in his shoulder wasn't as excruciating, but the wrong move still hurt like hell. He had to get out of here soon. He had a mission—to rid the world of scum like Falwell and Jenkins.

****

Lina met Sister Beatrice carrying the empty tray of food. "I finished making the tortillas, Sister."

"Thank you, Lina," the nun said. "Mr. Palermo is not at peace. He barely talked to me, only thanked me for the breakfast. He's so quiet, but not a peaceful quiet. More like he has a plan, and whatever his plan is makes him hard."

Lina sighed. His whole purpose was revenge. Jack didn't think of anything else. She wished she could find a way to lead him down a better path, a real path to peace. Taking another person's life was not going to bring him serenity. Why couldn't he understand?

"I'd better return to the kitchen," Sister Beatrice said.

"I'll say good morning. My class starts in fifteen

minutes," Lina said.

She gave a quick knock on the door and opened it. "Good morning," she said.

Jack didn't greet her before he spoke. "I have to get out of here," Jack said. "Can you help me?'

"Help you? How?" Lina's stomach flip-flopped. "Doc Sullivan said you could leave."

"I can. However, I'm not as strong as I'd like to be. I don't have a horse. Do you have horses here?"

"No, we don't. We only have a mule to pull the cart," Lina said. "There is a livery nearby. They might be able to help you."

"Horses cost money." Jack swallowed coffee. "How many saloons does this town have?"

"I don't frequent saloons, Mr. Palermo." Lina frowned.

He shook his head, scowling. "Of course not. Don't you know what businesses the town has?"

"How come you don't know?"

"I'd just arrived when I was shot, and the next thing I know I'm here," Jack said. "Didn't have time to look around much."

"Oh." Jack did exude a restlessness. The tension showed in the rigidness of his body and the tight grip on his cup.

"Do you think you can take me to the nearest saloon? I have to find someone," Jack said.

"The Five Star Saloon is on Old Cheyenne Road, back of us. You can walk," Lina said.

"I can. But I don't want to take a chance I might fall."

Lina's heart palpitated. "I'll have to take Alejandro with me. I can't be alone with you in public."

"Why not?" Jack stood and, after an unsteady wobble, managed to stay on his feet. He groaned in pain as he walked toward her. "I'm not too dangerous right now, though I can be." He raised his hand and caressed her cheek.

She stepped away quickly. "Please, I'm—I…"

Jack returned to sit on the bed. "Not a good idea. In more ways than one. I'll have to practice."

"Practice?"

"Walking." He grinned.

Lina took a deep breath. "Your wound is healing. Please be careful when you leave."

"I'll be careful. There's others who should be careful, too, once I leave this place," Jack muttered.

Lina touched the bandage, dry now instead of soaked with blood as it would get. Jack grabbed her hand.

"I want to kiss you, Lina," he said.

Her heart traveled to her throat, and she couldn't speak.

Jack opened his legs and pulled her close. "Lean down and let me kiss you, darling."

Lina couldn't breathe. She stooped to get close to Jack's face. He kissed her gently. She sighed. He kissed her again, his lips with a touch more pressure on them. A feeling of warmth engulfed her, and she placed her hands on his shoulders. Jack sensed her signal of acceptance, stood, and encircled her waist with his good arm. His lips caressed and moved on hers until she stopped thinking. Feelings of warmth, of happiness, and of an emotion or desire she couldn't name filled her senses when his body pressed on hers. Her body tingled as he touched her, and his was hard and strong. Her arms reached up to touch his hair with her hands, sliding the strands through her fingers. Her senses filled with his kiss, his touch… He ended the kiss. She couldn't face him.

Jack sat. "So when can you take me to the saloon?"

Still in a daze, Lina couldn't understand his question. "Saloon?"

He took her hand and kissed her palm. "Yeah."

"Oh. I have to go to my class now. We can go after school, around one, later today," she said. "I must go." She grabbed Jack's empty cup and left.

Outside the room, she sagged onto the wall. What had she done? She was a young woman—and unmarried. Kisses were not allowed unless a betrothal had been agreed to with her parents. Lina had none living. Who could give Jack permission to kiss her—or approve a betrothal? She was alone. However, she'd experienced her very first kiss, and she would not be remorseful.

Chapter 4

Jack had been going to the Five Star Saloon for two days. He had to lie low, not bring attention to himself. By eavesdropping, he found out the sheriff had retired and the new one was Branch Wylder. Just what he needed. A mama's boy with the town name as sheriff. The man was probably only a fixture. He had to find out who wielded power in this damn town. Keep out of their way. He'd stay out of the new sheriff's way, too. Until he found out more information. The bartender, Sonny Cash, kept to his bar. Jack ordered a beer. His money was dwindling. He'd have to find a way to make more.

Walking slowly—his body still hurt when he moved too fast, and he didn't want to bring attention to himself—Jack inched toward a table in a corner. He sat drinking his beer, surveying the patrons. Cowboys at tables sat playing poker, several men dressed in work clothes stood at the bar drinking, and a whore or two waited here and there with men who would soon disappear upstairs. The piano tinkled, and smells of sweat and beer filled his nostrils. Smoke from cigars curled slowly up to the ceiling.

A man seated alone a couple of tables over looked up. Jack stared. What the hell? Rufus McClintock? He'd believed the man long gone with Falwell and Jenkins.

Rufus must have sensed trouble, because he jerked his head up from taking a swallow of beer and stood rigid, his hand at his gunbelt. Jack stood and moved toward him.

"Jack? Is that you, man? We killed you." Rufus' voice rasped.

Jack shoved a pistol in the man's back, using his right hand. The pain in his shoulder jolted him, but he hung on. He grabbed Rufus by the neck and hauled him out the back door to the alley.

Rufus squirmed, and with the pain Jack suffered, he had to let him go. But not before he switched the gun to his left hand. He could shoot with it, but not as well.

"What the hell?" Rufus was older than Jack by twelve years, a freeman and Irish, taller than Jack by three inches, broad and muscular. The man personified a scary sight, especially at night in an alley. "I thought we done killed you."

Jack didn't give a damn at the man's confusion. "I'm not a ghost, *cabrón*. You left me for dead. *Chingado!* If I could, I'd beat you to a pulp, then shoot you and leave you in the cold to die."

"Jack? You were dead, man. I checked you." Rufus held out his arms.

Jack stepped back. "What? Are you going to pretend you're glad to see me? Yeah, and my scum of a sire was the best father this world has ever known."

"I never went along with what Falwell and Jenkins wanted to do," Rufus said, his voice hoarser than usual. "I loved Jimmy, man. You know that."

Jack couldn't see his face clearly in the dark, but he could hear the emotion in his voice.

"Those two-bit thieving murderers would have killed me, too, with no qualms," Rufus said. "I think they planned to. That's why I sneaked out while they slept, and I've been holed up in a cave across the Medicine Bow River."

Jack laughed without mirth. "You son-of-a-bitch. You expect me to believe you walk over here every day for a drink? That's a long haul to walk when you're hiding." He hadn't seen a river in this damned town, but he taunted Rufus anyway.

"Man, I got crazy by myself. I miss Texas. Too much cold and snow in these parts," Rufus said. "I was stuck for three weeks in that damn cave. My food ran out. I took to eating twigs just to have something to chew on."

Jack didn't comment on the man's woes. He could care less. "Where are Falwell and Jenkins? I have a score to settle with them. They have to pay for trying to kill me and, for damn sure, for killing my little brother."

"I don't know, Jack." Rufus stood straight as an arrow. "They hightailed it out of town because the Texas Rangers were after them. The banker at Cheyenne notified the sheriff there, and they called on the Rangers."

"They took all the money," Jack said. "Not even a few dollars for our trouble."

"I think the loot is buried somewhere here in Wylder. They had to travel light," Rufus said. "I'm sorry, Jack. I—well…" The man took out a handkerchief and blew his nose.

"Spare me your sympathy," Jack said. "I sure as hell don't need it. I don't need you. I need information. Where are those bastards headed?"

"I didn't wait around to find out. They did say they were going to try and outrun the Rangers and then trace back and get the money. But I don't know when." Rufus waved his hand.

Jack still had the gun pointed at him. Needles of excruciating pain pierced his shoulder, and despite the cold night, sweat dripped down his face. "Don't move." His legs were wobbly, and he wanted to sit.

"Kill me if you want, Jack," Rufus said. "All I have to look forward to is runnin', and I'm tired."

Jack wavered, and Rufus ran and held him up. He took Jack's gun and jammed it back in his holster. "Come on. Let's go inside."

Jack wanted to protest, but he didn't have the strength. Maybe Doc had been right. He should have taken more time to heal. Lina had tried to warn him, too. The thought of the young woman made him smile. He ached to see her, shy and hesitant, if only to tease her. She didn't know how to kiss, but he could teach her. Her goodness called out to him. Made him yearn for a better life. And then what? Hell, he'd never have better, only bad. He'd learned the lesson a long time ago.

Inside the saloon once again, Rufus helped him to a chair.

"You could have let me fall to the ground and left me there again, *cabrón*," Jack said, not feeling at all grateful for the man's assistance. Rufus had betrayed him.

He and Rufus and Old Man Clemens, who had established the Falwell-Jenkins outfit years ago, had formed a hesitant union against the Falwell brothers. Bruce "Buzzard" Falwell led the outfit with his younger brother, Houston "Jugbutt" Jenkins as partner. Houston had taken his ma's name. Any mention of his Falwell sire caused colorful foul language to emerge from Jugbutt's mouth, and he refused to use the man's name.

"Yeah, I could, but I didn't," Rufus said. "I left you the last time because you were dead, I swear, Jack."

Jack stared at the man, strong, big, but his face carried deep lines of weariness, and he looked as if he hadn't slept in weeks. Holed up in a cave, he probably hadn't.

Jack sighed. "I'm going to kill them. Are you with me?"

"Hell, yeah." Rufus finished his beer. "You bet."

Jack nodded and swallowed his beer. He stood. "I'll be in touch."

****

Lina stopped the cart by the Wylder mercantile. Alejandro and Hortencia were with her. Every month, the orphanage received their allotment from the diocese to buy groceries and supplies for the schoolroom. However, she and everyone had been busy with the different tasks needed to run the church, the kitchen, and the schoolroom, so time had gotten away and it was mid-March.

"Can we get candy, Miss Lina?" Hortencia asked with a hopeful smile.

Lina's heart wrenched. She wished she could give these children everything they wanted, but all she and the church could manage was the most basic of food and shelter.

"Not this time," Lina said.

Hortencia's smile faded.

"However, I'm going to buy flour, and I'll ask Sister Anne if we can bake sugar cookies. How about that?"

The little girl grinned. Alejandro stayed quiet. He knew better than to ask for what he couldn't have. The boy reminded her of Jack. Already, he'd had a hard life at barely thirteen years old.

Lina hadn't seen Jack since he'd kissed her, three days ago. She wondered where he'd gone. She jumped out of the cart and held up her hands to help Hortencia down. Alejandro jumped off the cart on the other side.

"I'm going to walk around," he said.

"Don't dawdle. I won't take long to buy what we need," Lina said.

He pushed his hat down and nodded. Lina watched as the slender boy walked away, his thin shoulders slumped. The only time she saw him happy was when he infrequently sang in church, and he refused to join the choir.

"Let's go inside, Miss Lina." Hortencia pulled at Lina's hand.

Lina turned her attention back to the child, took her hand, and walked up to the mercantile.

Finn Wylder smiled at Lina as she entered. Una Barlow, a plump woman with pinched lips, gathered her dress close to her as if Lina would soil her by walking near her. She ignored the woman. Having had run-ins with her before, Lina hoped today she would keep her mouth closed.

"How can I help you today, Miss Lina?" Mr. Wylder asked.

She handed him her list. "I—I need supplies for the church."

"All right. Give me a few minutes." He took her list and turned away to start putting her order on the counter.

The woman harrumphed. Lina ignored her and examined the bolts of fabric.

"Catholic orphan's hands touching the cloth ladies will buy," the woman muttered.

Grant me patience, God. I will regret what I say. And no one will benefit.

"Miss Lina, look at this," Hortencia said.

Lina turned, and the girl had dragged a doll as tall as her over to show Lina. She admitted the blonde-haired doll in a red dress with a black belt was beautiful, but she feared she'd break or get dirty. Then she'd have to pay for it.

"Oh, Hortencia," Lina said and took the doll. "Don't touch anything." Lina put the doll back on a higher shelf. "I'm sorry, Mr. Wylder."

"No harm done." He smiled. She noticed his brown eyes were kind.

Not the plump woman's. She glared at Lina.

"You should go back to Texas," she said. "That's where your kind belong."

"I've lived in Wylder since I was twelve years old, ma'am," Lina said. "I don't know anywhere else."

The woman harrumphed again. "Mr. Wylder, you should be more restrictive about who you allow to shop in your store."

"I wish I could, Mrs. Barlow," the man said and gave an imperceptible wink at Lina. "I wish I could."

She turned away to hide her smile.

Mr. Wylder helped Lina load the cart with the supplies. Alejandro returned and helped, too.

"Thank you, Mr. Wylder," Lina said.

"You're welcome, Miss Lina." He saluted her. "I'll see you next month."

Before Lina could climb back onto the wagon, Jack sauntered up.

"Need any help?"

Lina's heart somersaulted. "No, thank you. I'm

headed back to the church."

"I'd be glad if you'd give me a ride," he said. "I'm headed that way, too. The padre let me stay in the barn until I find a place to stay—or leave."

"Oh. I didn't know you were still—there," she said. "I hadn't seen you."

"Did you miss me?" He grinned.

Lina's body warmed at his words, and she didn't know what to say. Yes, she'd missed him, but she could never tell him.

"Miss Lina, let's go. I want to bake cookies." Hortencia's voice managed to clear her head.

"Jump in the back," Lina said. "We have to return to the church."

Without another word, Jack helped her climb back up to the cart seat and slowly got on the back of the cart where Alejandro rode as well.

Lina urged the mule on up Wylder Street and turned left on Sidewinder Lane, heading past the Outdoor Theater and Jake's Place, a restaurant she'd never eaten in and probably never would. Turning left again, this time onto Old Cheyenne Road, they rode by the Five Star Saloon. She kept going up to Backstreet, where St. Thomas Catholic Church was located.

As they'd traveled, she heard Jack and Alejandro talking.

"How long you been at the orphanage?" Jack asked.

"Practically all my life, seems like," Alejandro answered. "I was five when the woman who gave birth to me abandoned me."

"Hard life," Jack said.

"There's no other kind," Alejandro said.

Lina's heart broke at hearing the boy's words. Tears

filled her eyes. She'd lost her parents as a child, but she remembered the love of her parents. Her father, average height and thin as a rail, had worked all day in the cotton fields. In the evenings, Mami, who was as round as she was tall, cooked delicious meals. Lina remembered those evenings of joy and love and laughter that lived in her heart to this day. Papi would also play the guitar he'd named "Norma" and sing.

Hortencia yelled, "Sing, Alejandro. You'll be happy."

"Not today, Hortencia," Alejandro said. "I don't want to."

"You never want to," the little girl said. "I think if you sang all the time you'd be happy all the time."

Lina couldn't find fault with her logic. What prevented Alejandro from singing? If she could, Lina would sing the songs her father sang, but she couldn't remember the words, only the strumming of the guitar and the sound of her father's voice.

Jack remained quiet. What were his thoughts? Probably only about killing and getting revenge for his attempted murder and his little brother's death. The road he'd chosen would lead him to more sadness and death. He would never be happy.

****

Because Jack wanted to be near Lina yesterday after he'd helped her and the children haul the supplies inside the church and kitchen, he took off and went in search of Rufus and his cave. The man had given him directions. He said to cross the train tracks, go down Copper Alley by the stockyards, down to Bone Orchard Road, go right to the Wylder Bridge. A little way from the bridge was a pathway to the cave he'd found—not really a cave made of stone, but a hillside worn out by weather and water through the years.

Jack had arrived last night. He'd been tired out from the long walk, thanked Rufus, and spread out a blanket he'd borrowed from the church and promptly went to sleep.

Now, he woke to the sound of the river gushing nearby. Rufus sat outside the opening of the cave near a fire. Jack couldn't stifle a groan when he moved. His body ached from the hard ground, and he was chilled. His shoulder hurt, too, and he thought of the soft bed at the orphanage.

"I got coffee. You want some?" Rufus asked.

"Yeah." Jack accepted the cup of coffee offered—bitter, but hot.

"How'd you sleep?" Rufus drank.

"I've slept in worse places," Jack said, remembering when he and Jimmy lived on the streets. He hated to dwell on those times. He'd given his little brother a hard life, but he had consoled himself with the knowledge that both he and Jimmy would be dead if not worse if they'd stayed around their father. Yet Jimmy had died anyway.

"I know that," Rufus said. "Yep, I do."

"I walked around town yesterday, hoping to hear word of Falwell and Jenkins. Damn hard to get information when you don't know who to ask and who's watching." Jack moved his right shoulder to smooth out the stiffness. Sleeping on hard cold ground was probably not the best way to go. If Doc saw him, for sure he'd glare at him. Jack had a feeling the man had lived as hard a life as him. Nobody came out West for the scenery.

"Did you find out who the sheriff is?"

"Branch Wylder. No one knows his history.

However, I heard he takes no nonsense from rowdy cowboys shooting their guns off in town and scaring the ladies and children. He's at the saloons before anybody can count to three if he hears there's trouble. I was wrong about him," Jack said.

"How?" Rufus stretched his hands to the fire.

"I wondered how a man who had the same name as the town would be as sheriff. Thought him a puppet."

Rufus stood and stretched his legs. "I know we ran across a lot of those kinds of lawmen through the years. There's them who get paid to look the other way. Not necessarily in your favor." Rufus chuckled, but the merriment didn't reach his dark, angry eyes.

Jack nodded and finished the coffee. "Any more left?" The hot liquid, though not tasty, warmed him.

"A bit." Rufus poured the remainder from the pan.

"We need horses, Rufus," Jack said. "I don't have a red cent. I'd hoped the church would have at least one, but all they have is an old mule."

"We could go up close to the mountains and see if we can snag a wild one," Rufus said.

"Man, I haven't tamed a horse in ages. Besides, in my shape, I'd be trampled to death before I could kill Falwell." Jack frowned.

"Maybe at the mines?" Rufus suggested.

"Mines?"

"Yep, they's a coal mine a ways out of Wylder toward the Medicine Bow Mountains."

Jack shrugged. "We work in the coal mines to get money for horses?"

"Nope." Rufus doused the fire. "We go over and check for desperate faces. The work is hard, and people lose hope very quick up there. They're willing to sell all their worldly goods to get out of that place. Of course, many times the horses are taken up by the mine owners. Depends."

"Seems too chancey," Jack said.

"You got any ideas?"

"I found out a horse at the livery cost sixty dollars," Jack said.

"Man. Might as well be six hundred dollars."

"Maybe we should go work at the coal mine," Jack said.

"We could ask for work at the grist mill," Rufus said. "They pay some over two dollars a day, maybe two fifty."

"It'll take three weeks to earn money for one horse. And that's if the livery has sixty-dollar horses. For all we know, while we're working the price will go up," Jack said. Frustration and anger filled him. After all these years, he had zero. For the first time in his life, he contemplated the future. Totally stupid, since once he killed Falwell, he'd hang. No future there.

"You got a better idea?" Rufus crossed his arms, a sure sign the man was angry.

Jack laughed and realized he'd missed this fellow. Memories of sitting around a campfire with him, Old Man Clemens and Jimmy singing, filled him. The Falwell brothers would always go into town to the saloons. Jack did too, on occasion, but he didn't like to leave his little brother alone too much, though he knew the other two men would watch over him.

"Guess not," Jack said. "Let's get to work."

Chapter 5

Lina sneaked out the back door from the kitchen. Hopefully, Sister Anne wouldn't come and lock up. If she did, Lina didn't know what she'd do to get back inside. She needed to find out if Jack took her up on her offer to stay in the barn. Father Pete had said Jack would be welcome. The church catered to orphans of all ages.

She leaned against the wall of the church and gauged the distance to the barn. Could she run fast enough so no one would see her? She crossed herself and took a chance. She opened the barn door and stepped inside.

Large hands grabbed her around the waist. She opened her mouth to scream, but a strong arm pulled her against his chest.

Jack!

She leaned closer to him and let her body melt against him. Words from the nuns, Bible verses, and Father Pete's sermons reverberated through her brain.

This is wrong, Lina. You're committing a sin. Marriage comes before intimacy with a man.

"God, I missed you," Jack said. Then his warm lips sought hers, and she was aware only of him. He held her with just one hand around her waist. She put both her arms around his neck and caressed his hair. His beard grazed the tender skin around her mouth and her cheeks, but she didn't care, and when he kissed her until she opened her mouth, his tongue delved in.

"Oh…" The word ended in a moan.

"I want to touch you, but I can use only one hand," he said before his mouth covered hers again.

She had two hands, and she used them to touch him all over—his hair, the nape of his neck, his muscled back and shoulders. He pushed her closer to him and a hardness between her upper thighs made her jump. He caressed her hips.

"Oh…you must not… I must not…" Lina said the words, but she didn't tell him to stop. Warmth engulfed her. Her legs wobbled with emotion, and she sagged against Jack.

Jack held her close. "We can't. You're right. I'm not here to stay."

Lina, too wrapped up in her emotions, barely heard him. Her arms stayed holding him, touching him.

Jack walked backward, keeping her in his arms, and brought her down to the floor. He leaned back against a post.

She sat on his lap and kept her head on his shoulder, not his injured one. Her arms were around his neck. She sighed, long and broken. Her body shook.

"Are you cold?" Jack moved his hand up and down her arm vigorously.

"No, I—I feel very warm." She kept her eyes closed, not wanting to wake up from this wonderful dream. Because this was a dream. This could not be happening—to her—a penniless orphan whose life up to now had been work—classroom, kitchen, and an empty bed. She had been grateful, first for Father Bellamy so many years ago when he took pity on her, then for Father Pete. He'd allowed her to stay and teach when she reached maturity and should have left. Nothing, however, had ever made her feel so wanted and so—loved.

Did Jack love her? Of course he did. A man wouldn't kiss a woman with such passion without love in his heart. She was wary, however, about asking him and about saying words she instinctively knew he would not like to hear from her. She decided to tease him. She opened her eyes and touched his beard.

"Your beard makes you look very handsome, but—ummm—makes my face itch." She laughed. "Does your face itch?"

He chuckled. "No, my whiskers keep my face warm."

She giggled and raised her head.

Jack kissed her, and soon they were kissing again as if they hadn't decided to stop.

"*Ay,* Lina, you'll be the death of me," he said. His arm tightened around her.

"You have flour all over yourself. Were you baking?" She giggled again due to Jack. She'd never giggled in her life—well, maybe as a little girl.

"I'm working at the grist mill. I need money for a horse," he said.

"I wish I had a horse. I would give him—or her to you." She leaned against him again.

"I know you would," he said.

"Are you still looking for revenge?"

He didn't answer for what seemed like several minutes. She wished she hadn't asked. Revenge had been all he'd talked about while in bed with his gunshot wound.

"Yeah," he said.

"I wish—I wish…" She touched his injured

shoulder. "How are you working with your shoulder bandaged up and in a sling? Are you still in pain?"

Jack gave a small sigh, probably glad she'd stopped talking about his revenge.

"Not as much anymore, but I have to work. I take the sling off while I'm working. They wouldn't hire a man who couldn't give his all to the task."

"Do you check the bandage for bleeding?"

"Yeah, Lina, I do. I've been careful. I can't afford more setbacks," he said.

She put both arms around his waist.

"Thank you for not talking about the revenge. I know you don't understand, but I have to do what's right, to honor my little brother. He didn't deserve to die. I did. I do."

"You don't either, but I know you won't believe me."

"I'd better get back to the cave. It's getting darker and darker."

"I wish you'd stay in the barn. The barn is still cold, but at least you'll have cover if the wind blows or we get a snowstorm again," Lina said. "Snow doesn't stop falling sometimes until April."

"I don't want to endanger you, or the church, or the kids. I'm after very dangerous men," he said.

Fear engulfed Lina as Jack's kisses had a short time ago. Fear didn't make her body tingle pleasantly, though. It filled her with sorrow for Jack and for the life that had led him to this point. She decided to pray for him. God listened to sinners. Tonight, she'd really sinned.

Jack helped her to her feet once he stood. He held her tightly.

"Take care of yourself, Jack."

He held her close, then kissed her lightly. "I will. Good night, *amor*."

Jack led her back to the church and the kitchen door. Lina walked in and leaned against the door. He'd called her "love."

****

The next morning, Jack woke to the smell of coffee again. Rufus always woke before he did. Maybe he shouldn't take revenge alone. Falwell was liable to find him asleep and kill him.

He remembered kissing Lina last night. She was so innocent he could have had his way with her before she realized what was happening. He'd never been slow with a woman. Then again, he'd never been with virgins. Lina, a really young woman in so many ways, had him in knots. This had never happened to him before.

From the time he'd escaped his abusive father with his little brother, he hadn't stopped to think. Survival was vital. Jimmy had been five years old, an age when he needed nurturing and the love of a mother. Jack had been thirteen, an age when his interest in girls would normally have appeared.

However, watching the way his father treated his mother had stanched any desire to have a wife. He'd probably be a bastard like his father. He would never, ever, put a woman in danger like that. By the time he and Jimmy left, Jack had only one purpose on his mind. Build a life miles away in another town with his little brother and forget he ever had a father. Memories of his gentle, beautiful mother did surface now and then. His first memory of her had been at Christmas. She'd worn a pale blue dress, and she'd arranged her black hair in curls on top of her head. She'd put a mantilla on like Lina wore, only his mother's had been made of lace, not cotton like Lina's. She'd sewn black trousers and white shirts for him and Jimmy. Jack smiled at the memory. He'd liked the way he looked. They'd walked to church and the service had not been as boring as usual, with the choir singing hymns he recognized. Jimmy had been four years old, but he already liked to sing. And he did with as much gusto as he could, though he hadn't known all the words.

Once they'd returned home, however, his father had greeted them in a belligerent tone and demanded his supper. Jack's mother had flung off her mantilla and hurried to set the table and put the meal on the table. Jack knew the moment his father would ruin the evening. Through narrowed eyes, he'd glared at his mother.

"Who in hell did you go see? I always knew you would cheat on me!"

Why the man would think his wife would cheat on him with her sons in tow was incomprehensible to Jack as a child. He still did not understand as an adult. He'd blocked out the rest of the night. The sight of pale blue dresses and curly black hair took him back to that Christmas night. By the end of the night, his mother's beauty had been erased. His new white shirt, and Jimmy's, were torn and bloodied. His father passed out on the floor amid the overturned table and the Christmas dinner.

"Hey, Jack. Come out and drink a cup of coffee," Rufus said. "Gettin' more bitter settin' on the fire."

Jack shook his head and realized where he was. "Coming. Stiffer this morning than others."

Rufus laughed. "You got soft sleeping in that orphanage bed."

Jack took the cup without another word. He stayed standing and looked out through unseeing eyes at the trees while he listened to the river gushing along.

"What's wrong, Jack?" Rufus stretched in front of the fire. "I plan to enjoy this day. No work. No flour all over myself. That damn flour gets everywhere, under my clothes, in my boots. I may jump in the river and take a bath."

Jack laughed. "About damn time, too."

"Oh, yeah? Since when did you take a bath?" Rufus ribbed him.

"Maybe I should. I need to douse myself with cold water."

"How so? You could always satisfy your itch at Miss Addie's," the man said.

Jack wondered if he should tell Rufus about Lina.

"My 'itch,' as you say, is not for the likes of Addie's girls. I—aw, forget it." Jack sat, holding his hands to the fire. He kept the sling on for as long as he could. He should have taken it off last night and really held on to Lina.

"Tell me," Rufus said.

"I met a woman at the orphanage," he said.

"I thought nobody but nuns lived there."

"I thought so, too. She may be the only one aside from the children. She's a teacher,"

"What's her name?" Rufus examined the bottom of his cup.

"Evangelina Gaitan. Lina," Jack said.

"Pretty name. Pretty girl?" Rufus asked. "Of course, she is. You always drew the eyes of the pretty ones. Made Falwell furious. Jugbutt, on the other hand, never met a woman he couldn't force to like him. Bastard."

Jack couldn't agree more.

"So?" Rufus probed.

"So, I don't trifle with virgins. With a woman like Lina. She expects marriage. She told me girls in her family get betrothed before they can be in the same room with a man."

"What's she doing in an orphanage if she has a family?"

Jack sighed. "She doesn't. She's been an orphan since she was twelve years old. The orphanage has been her home."

"Were you with her last night?"

When Jack didn't answer, Rufus grunted. "I heard you return after I'd been asleep for hours."

"I met her in the barn of the church," Jack said. "Spent time with her, talking, and so forth."

"And so forth? Never heard it called that before." Rufus grinned.

"I'm a gentleman," Jack said.

"You're not a gentleman, Jack, and we both know it. I do know you have respect for women no matter their station. I seldom come across a man like you. Never force a woman. Never lift a fist to her."

"I can't trust myself, Rufus. That's why I'll never marry a woman. I'm afraid I'll turn into my father."

"I don't think so," Rufus said. "I've told you that before. However, every man has to live his life the way he sees fit. Now, I have news."

Jack narrowed his eyes.

"Heard talk at the saloon last night. Falwell and Jenkins are either in town or coming in."

"They think I'm dead," Jack said. "Do you think they're looking for you?"

"Naw. Don't think so," Rufus said. "Those vermin won't bother me none now. They're probably glad to be rid of me. They know I can't blab to the law. Who would believe me?"

"So what do you think?"

"They're coming back to get the money. Wherever the damn hiding place is. I have no idea." Rufus poured out the remaining coffee in his cup to douse the fire. The smoke rose and disappeared into the air.

Jack stood and raised one arm. "Yeah. Day of reckoning is coming."

****

Lina squirmed on her seat while she waited in the cart with the old mule on Old Cheyenne Road. She'd escaped after mass and cajoled Sister Beatrice, a young nun and kind soul, to help her fill a basket for a picnic. In spite of feeling guilty for lying to her by saying she wanted to reflect by herself in the field nearby, her feelings for Jack were stronger. Lina hadn't told Sister Anne—the woman would see right through her. Lina couldn't go near the tree where they'd found Jimmy dead, but she'd found another tree several feet away. She wanted to invite Jack to go with her. Sunday was the only time she could be by herself with no questions. Jack didn't have to work at the mill, either.

Saloons were always open, so she waited for Jack. Maybe he would come by. What if he didn't? What if he was with one of Addie's girls? Or with another woman? What did she really know about him? He hadn't talked to her.

Her heart fluttered when she saw him cross the street. She called out to him, but he didn't hear. She tried again. "Jack?" She gave him a tentative wave.

He stopped, stared at the saloon, then at the ground. Slowly, he walked toward her.

"What are you doing here?"

Lina lowered her glance, then lifted her head to face him. "I waited for you because—because I want to invite you…" She licked her lips.

Jack's gaze never wavered.

She grinned. "You shaved a little of your beard off."

Jack's cheeks reddened. "Yeah, well, grew out too long. Needed to be trimmed."

Lina smiled. "You're more handsome."

"Thank you." Jack teased her. "What are you doing out here alone? Are you meeting your *novio*? Where's Alejandro?"

"I escaped. I asked Sister Beatrice to help me fix a picnic, and I want to invite you—invite you to eat with me," she said.

"All right." Jack jumped into the cart and took the reins. "Where are we going?"

"Go behind the church. There's a field and a tree," she said. "Not the same one where we found you and your brother, another one."

"Let me know when to stop," he said.

The chilly air breezed through her, but it was bearable.

When they reached the tree Lina had chosen, she said, "There. Stop there."

Jack jumped out of the cart and helped Lina out, then lifted the picnic basket from the back of the cart. She spread out a brown blanket over the grass under the tree in a section screened on three sides by smaller trees and bushes. Though now bereft of leaves, the cover still provided a feeling of seclusion. They could see out the fourth side to waves of dry grass.

"Is this our romantic secret place?" Jack asked.

Lina blushed, embarrassed. Her cheeks were hot to the touch when she raised her hand to cover her mouth. "I didn't mean—I'm sorry…"

"I'm teasing you, Lina. I haven't been on a picnic in a long time." He stopped her from wringing her hands in her lap. "What did you bring to eat? I'm hungry."

"Our best Sunday meal—fried chicken, mashed potatoes, gravy, and peas. Sister Beatrice also packed half a loaf of fresh-baked bread."

"A feast fit for a king," he said.

"Oh, and a jug of lemonade. Would you like some?" Lina poured the sweet beverage into two ceramic cups she'd wrapped in two separate cloths to keep them from breaking. The cups were kept in a cupboard and never used. Today was a special day, so she'd taken them, praying they wouldn't break. She'd have to confess and to pay for them with money she didn't have.

"Very good," Jack said. "Did you cook?"

"No, Sister Beatrice did. She makes the best." Lina filled two plates—Jack's with plenty to eat; for herself, only one piece of chicken and small portions of the other dishes. She wasn't sure she could eat with Jack present.

However, Jack ate with a voracious appetite, barely looking up at her until he'd finished. Lina ate more than she expected, since Jack had been so intent on his food rather than her.

"Do you want more?"

"Is there more?" Jack glanced at the open picnic basket.

"Yes. Two more pieces of chicken. You can have the rest of the potatoes and peas. The bread is gone, I'm afraid."

"Best meal I've had in a long time," he said. "Thank you."

Lina enjoyed sitting with Jack afterward, looking up at the sky, finishing off the lemonade.

Jack inched over to sit closer to her. He sat back against the tree and took off his sling.

"Come here, Lina."

She hesitated.

"Please."

She sat next to him by the tree.

He grinned. "Don't you want to sit on my lap?"

She blushed again. "Yes. I also want you to kiss me again."

Jack needed no further permission. He pulled her close, settled her on his lap, and kissed her. He tasted of lemonade. A smell of leather and musk filled her nostrils as well. She hoped she smelled like a garden like he'd said the other day in the orphanage. And not of chicken.

Before she realized what was happening, she was lying full length on the blanket with Jack. She should be afraid, but she wasn't. His hard, muscled body on top of hers made her want to inch closer. His mouth covered hers; his tongue filled her. Her arms were around him. Without conscious knowledge, she lifted his shirt and touched the body she'd dreamed of touching ever since she'd seen his bare chest. His body caressed hers. Again, hardness rubbed between her upper thighs, making her lower body move from side to side. She sighed.

"Aw, shit," Jack said. He sat up. "I have to leave. I'll take you back to the orphanage."

Lina sat up too. "Jack—Jack…" She heaved a sigh. Her heart ached. "What—what did I—do wrong?"

He pulled her close. "Not you, me. Lina, I'm not staying in this town. I can't take your virtue only to leave you."

He picked up the picnic basket. Lina pulled the blanket from the ground, folded it, and hugged it to her still-tingling body.

Outside the church barn, he said, "I'm sorry." He kissed her, long and hard, one more time and walked away.

Lina watched him until he disappeared from sight, on his way to the saloon and more experienced women.

Chapter 6

After her classes were over, Lina helped Sister Anne in the kitchen with baking bread for the week. They'd already made ten loaves and were waiting on the last two.

"Did you enjoy your picnic on Sunday?" Sister Anne asked as she washed the bowls, tins, and utensils they'd used for baking.

Lina smiled. "Yes, I did, very much."

Sister Anne banged a pot down.

Lina jumped. "I mean, I liked being outside with the trees and grass, though they haven't bloomed yet. I did do my reflections."

"Not, however, on your picnic," the nun said. "You did them once you returned to the orphanage."

Lina's heart beat faster. How did Sister Anne know? Who had spied on her? How would she punish her?

"You went to meet someone, didn't you? A man, perhaps? The gunfighter?"

Lina turned away to put a dry pot on a shelf above the dry sink.

"I will appreciate an honest answer, Lina, and more so if you do not lie to me again." Sister Anne's voice exuded suppressed anger.

"Yes, I met Jack Palermo. I should say, I waylaid him on his way to the saloon and invited him on a picnic with me." Lina couldn't face the nun, who up to now had

61

been very kind to her, if a bit gruff.

"Did he have his way with you?"

Lina remembered Jack's body lying on top of hers. And she'd ached for more than he gave her, an unidentifiable need—or desire.

"No, he didn't."

"Were you tempted?"

Lina faced Sister Anne. "Yes, I was. I've—been—tempted ever since I first saw him."

"I know." The nun splashed water on a pot to rinse the soap off. "That's why I limited your time with him. I didn't so much see the attraction in your eyes but in his. I know men, Lina. Er—I used to know them. I don't imagine they've changed much from when I knew them intimately."

What does Sister Anne mean? Hasn't she always been a nun?

"Never you mind what I mean. I can see you want to question me. I have my secrets, and that's how they'll stay," she said.

"I'm not remorseful," Lina said. "He wanted me. Maybe he can love me."

"If you think that man will love you, you are sadly mistaken. He's a gunfighter, an outlaw. You have no idea what kind of a man he is. What will happen to you if you persist in this is that he will leave you pregnant and alone. What are you, an unmarried woman, going to do with a child? That man is going down a destructive path. I don't have to know what's on his mind. I can see he's not at peace, and whatever he's decided will give him peace will not do so. I've met his kind before."

"You're right," Lina said.

"I'm right about what?" Sister Anne walked to the

wood-burning stove and took out the remaining two loaves of bread.

"He wants to avenge the death of his little brother and his own near-death," Lina said. "I've tried to convince him doing so will not make him feel better. He won't listen. Now, he won't talk to me about his plans."

"Have you fallen in love with him?" Sister Anne put her hands on Lina's shoulders.

Lina couldn't meet the nun's eyes, but then she raised her head. "Yes, I have, but I will never tell him. He won't know what to do if I do. I think he will feel guilty for paying attention to me. He'll feel sorry for me, and I won't stand for that. I don't want his pity."

"Yes, I know," the woman said and turned to flip the bread out of the tins to cool.

Lina threw a cloth over the loaves.

Sister Anne sat at the small table where they mixed the ingredients and absent-mindedly wiped the already-clean top surface. "I fell in love once, too."

Lina smiled. "Is this your secret story, Sister?"

Sister Anne frowned. "Don't you tell this to a living soul. Father Bellamy was aware. He was the one who found me at my lowest point and brought me here. I had no one. My family had disowned me. The man I loved had deserted me. He'd only been toying with me.

"I've always been on the plump side, you see. My sister was thin but shapely and had the most beautiful long blonde hair. My hair is this mousy brown color, always has been."

Sister Anne pulled a brown tress from under her habit and grimaced. "But then, Horace Dean came into my life. He was very tall, slender, not muscular like your Jack, but he had dark hair and blue eyes. I fell deeply in love. I believed he had, too. He asked my father if he could court me, and to my surprise, my father said yes. Horace and I went everywhere, appropriately chaperoned by my sister. I lived for the times I would see Horace.

"One day I'd been out shopping with my maid. I returned home to find Horace in the study with my father. I rushed in full of smiles to apologize for forgetting we'd made an appointment to meet and for making him wait. My sister stood in front of father's desk."

Sister Anne stood and scrubbed another bowl. Her shoulders shook. Was she crying? Or laughing? Lina stood to go to her and found she was doing both.

"In my happiness, I didn't notice right away that they held hands and were standing very close together. You see, they'd gone in to tell my father they were in love and wanted to get married. The only way they'd been able to figure out to see each other was to pretend Horace was interested in me. They could no longer hide their feelings.

"My father took their side. He told me I had to step aside. My sister's happiness was important. My father said I shouldn't expect Horace to be with a woman he didn't love. When my sister left the room on Horace's arm, she turned to me and smirked. She didn't love Horace. She wanted to take him away from me. My only consolation—my revenge, I guess you could say—was that Horace was going to be as unhappy as I was."

"Oh, Sister Anne," Lina said.

"I don't want your pity, like you don't want mine. I attended parties and drank too many champagne goblets until my father sent me to an aunt in a nearby town. I ran away and returned to my father's house.

"My father heard of a matchmaker who arranged marriages with men in the West. He made one without my knowledge and sent me here to Wylder, Wyoming. The man, a widower, said he needed a helpmate to run his farm and tend his two children. While working in his field, I fainted. The doctor—not Doc Sullivan, another one—said I was pregnant."

Sister Anne paused, then sat at the table again.

"Were you?"

"I'd been intimate with Horace. The man told me I'd betrayed him. The next morning, he stuffed my clothes in a suitcase and set it outside. He demanded I leave before the children woke up.

"Instead of going to the priest as I should have, since I'd been raised Catholic, I decided to show everyone I could resolve the situation. So I looked for work. No one would hire me. I didn't know how to do anything. I'd been taught to embroider and to draw, along with the etiquette to catch a husband. I worked in a brothel. Not Miss Addie's. I didn't want anyone to know, here in Wylder."

"What happened to your baby?" Lina tried not to appear shocked, but for Sister Anne, the wielder of discipline and organization, to have this secret stunned her.

"I miscarried," the nun said. "After that, I stopped caring. Until I got beaten so bad I ran away. Father Bellamy found me on the road to Wylder. I'd been on my way back to him. He took me in, provided care and shelter. When I healed, he let me work here. I did anything I could to be useful. Much like you, Lina. Until I received the calling to be a nun."

Sister Anne patted her on the shoulder. "Don't let a man's flowery words lead you down the wrong path. If he wants to marry you, then by all means do so. If all he wants is to pass the time of day with you, leave him. Life is hard for everyone, especially when you don't have money, but more so for a woman alone."

"I'll be careful, Sister," Lina said. "Thank you for telling me your story. I'll try to benefit from your wisdom. I don't want to do anything to jeopardize my life. If my life here in the orphanage is threatened, I won't have anywhere else to go, just like you didn't."

In spite of Sister Anne's bluntness and occasional harshness, she was a kind soul life had scarred. Lina hugged her. "God loves you. I do, too."

Lina returned to drying the dishes after Sister Anne washed them.

****

Jack hadn't seen Lina since their picnic last Sunday. He didn't have to work at the grist mill, but he couldn't go see Lina, either. He remembered the fried chicken fondly. Since he and Rufus had been working, they had money to buy a few groceries like bread and canned goods to heat over the fire. The river also had fish they'd been able to catch now and then. Neither one of them were experts.

Jack remembered Lina at the picnic. He wished he could see her in a colorful dress, or anything else except those gray shapeless dresses she wore. However, after touching her more than once now, he'd found she had very shapely curves underneath. He threw a rock toward the river. He hated waiting around, but he had no choice at the moment. He couldn't very well go traipsing into town and take a chance on being seen. Rufus, however, came and went effortlessly, though he kept out of the way and hid in the crowds as much as he could. He kept his eyes peeled for the Falwell-Jenkins outfit and his ears alert to hear any news of their return. So far, no news.

He'd settled against the wall of the cave to try and sleep when he heard footsteps on rustling leaves. He cocked his pistol and inched over to the mouth of the cave. He saw Rufus coming. He had a bag in his hand.

"Hey, Jack, you here?" Rufus called out to him. "I have sweets for the sweet." The man laughed.

"What are you talking about?" Jack crawled out of the cave and stood, glad for the company. He'd been going crazy with his thoughts about Falwell and Lina, two very different things.

"I went to see the livery owner. Soon, we'll have enough for one horse between the two of us. I figured I'd find out if we could work out a deal. But no dice. He wants all the money at once. I don't blame him."

Jack knew that, too. Why had Rufus asked?

"However, he gave me good news. There's a widow who lives about two miles outside of Wylder, and she has two horses."

"We need two horses, but we won't have the money until near the end of the month." Jack eyed the bag. The smell of sugar and cinnamon made his mouth water. He didn't care much for sweets too often, but he hadn't eaten any for a long time now. "What's in the bag?"

"Listen, Jack, these horses are not what you'd expect, but I figured we could get 'em for now since we need 'em so bad. I'm damn tired of walkin' back and forth to town. But—I went to visit this widow, and them horses are the poorest kind of horseflesh I've seen in years." Rufus laughed.

Jack frowned. "If they were so bad, why you acting like a fool? Did you fall in love with this widow?"

"No, man. She's old," Rufus said.

"You're old," Jack said, uncaring if he hurt the man's feelings.

"I've got a few more years on me than you, but I ain't that old," he said. "I told her I had to talk to my partner and we'd get back to her. She'd been baking, and she offered these sweets. I already ate a couple with her, with coffee. Good. Good." Rufus finally put his hand in the bag and pulled out a thick slice of cinnamon bread. "Will you look at that?" Rufus grinned.

Jack's mouth watered, but he hesitated.

"Good. When I told her I had a partner, she put in extra."

"Partner?" Jack glared at Rufus. "Partners don't leave each other dead in the cold."

"Aw, shit," Rufus said. "I told you I thought you were dead. I fired another shot into the ground to assure Falwell I'd made sure you were dead, because I couldn't put a bullet in you. Jack, I, well, I…" He threw the bag on the ground. "Eat 'em or throw 'em away."

Jack watched the man go toward the bridge. His steps were slower than they used to be. He saw him take out his handkerchief. Again, he remembered the nights by the campfire—him, Jimmy, Old Man Clemens, and Rufus. He could have gone into town, too. The girls in the saloons liked him because he was tall, strong, and yeah, attractive. But he'd preferred to stay behind. He had loved Jimmy, Jack realized.

Jack yelled, "Hey, Rufus, I'm sorry."

Rufus waved his hand but didn't return.

Jack sat on his haunches, picked up the bag, and

took the cinnamon bread out. The feel and smell of the bun reminded him of the ones his mother had baked. They tasted like a memory, too.

He ran after Rufus after he'd finished a second chunk of bread and put the bag on a high rock, where he hoped the varmints would stay away.

Rufus sat on the dry grass by the river.

"What about those horses the old widow has?"

Rufus stared out into the distance but didn't say a word.

Jack sighed and threw himself on the cold ground. "I was angry. Then, I was hurt and betrayed—by you. Yeah, not the kind of emotions an outlaw should feel. I believed I'd gotten hard enough not to feel anything except for Jimmy. My being soft—that's what gave my father so much pleasure in beating me when I was a boy."

Rufus said, "I envied you—you and Jimmy—no matter what, you had each other. Falwell and Jenkins do, too, but not in the same way. They'd turn on each other at the drop of a hat if the price was right. I was happy to be a part of your life."

Jack held out his hand. "All's forgotten between us. I won't bring the past up again."

Rufus took it and stood. "Let's go see those horses before night comes."

****

Lina sat at her desk in front of the class. She'd given the children a reading assignment from their readers. She noticed Alejandro would glance at the book, then stare out the window. He never talked to her like the other children. Then, again, he really wasn't a child. He was thirteen years old, considered a young man. He should be studying a trade and getting ready to support himself.

The poor child had no family, as far as she knew. He'd been in the orphanage for eight years, and she doubted anyone would show up and claim him after such a long time.

She made up her mind. Before Easter arrived, she was going to talk to Alejandro, find out what interested him. Maybe she could speak to the business owners in Wylder and ask if they could take on an apprentice. The only thing he'd ever shown interest in was the train. Whenever he couldn't be found at the orphanage, they ran to the edge of the street and up Old Cheyenne Road, and they'd see him walking along the train tracks. He would talk to the train conductor and the other workers there. Lina promised herself she'd find out and help Alejandro. Life could be hard with no one around who cared.

Lina admitted living at the orphanage all these years made her feel part of a family. Father Pete, Sister Anne, and Sister Beatrice were people she could turn to if she needed to. The Mother Superior ruled behind the scenes; Lina never interacted with her on a regular basis. However, she was a fair leader and knowledgeable on assigning work to help the orphanage run smoothly.

Hortencia raised her hand, and Lina went to her desk.

"I need help with a word. I don't know how to say it," the little girl said.

"Let me see," Lina said. "Point out the word to me." She stayed a few minutes to help.

Before she returned to her desk, Lina glanced around the class to check if anyone else needed assistance. Alejandro raised his head and opened his mouth to speak, but he gave her a half-hearted smile and went back to his book. Of course, if he had a problem, he wouldn't talk to her.

What kind of situation did she have with Jack? Maybe she hoped for too much in their few encounters. He'd kissed her, and while she wanted to believe he'd been sincere, she wasn't sure. He'd probably had many women in his life. Lina might be innocent, but she saw things in town and had heard of the Wylder County Social Club and Miss Addie. Men liked women, and not always for marriage.

Lina didn't have any family protection, so the only person who could protect her was herself. She winced. She'd failed miserably with Jack. She'd let him kiss her, touch her in places only a husband should, and had laid down with him—outside. *Ay, Dios mio! Why did I do so?*

She must have been louder than she'd meant to, because several students raised their heads. concern in their eyes.

Hortencia asked, "Are you in pain, Miss Lina?"

This time Lina stifled her groan. "No, Hortencia, I'm fine. I think reading time is over. Let's take out our slates and do arithmetic."

The whole class muttered or sighed. Lina smiled. Maybe they'd forget she'd been sitting at her desk making noises.

Chapter 7

Jack walked with Rufus toward Cheyenne. The widow lived about two miles out. After several nights sleeping in a cold cave on hard ground, Jack's body hurt.

"Not as easy to sleep on the ground anymore, is it?" Rufus asked. He walked more slowly than Jack.

Jack wanted to voice a denial, but nodded. "No other choice, Rufus."

The cold air kept them moving, and soon Jack didn't feel the chill. He actually began to feel too warm and would have taken his duster off, but then he would have had to carry the damn thing.

"Seen Lina lately?" Rufus asked.

Jack's heart jumped. He debated whether or not to answer Rufus and decided to do so. "No."

They walked on the dirt road that led to Cheyenne. It usually saw traffic going by stagecoach or train, not on foot.

The tracks lay to the right side of them. Dry grass and brittle trees lined the land on both sides.

"I can't see her. My life is uncertain. Hell, I might be dangling from a tree in the next few days, when Falwell and Jenkins come into town. I have nothing to give her. Living in an orphanage is not ideal, but at least she has a warm place to stay and food to eat every day. With me, all she'll get is a miserable life."

Rufus remained quiet. They walked without

speaking.

"Do you remember when we were in Fort Worth for near three months after we worked on that cattle drive? We had money to burn. We lived in a hotel. Man, I wish I'd kept part of that money now. Truth be told, through the years, I wish I'd put a few of those damn dollars aside for a rainy day—or a snowy day." Rufus laughed. "Anyways, do you recall a lady by the name of Bertina?"

Jack glanced at Rufus. The man's face had softened, and his eyes had a faraway dazed look. He vaguely remembered a tall, slender woman with olive skin and dark brown curly hair. She'd owned a dress shop in town and always wore the prettiest dresses Jack had ever seen, aside from his mother's.

"Sort of," he said.

"I spent my time with her. She cooked meals for me, kept my socks darned, sewed on buttons on my shirts. She made me a pair of trousers." Rufus chuckled. "I think that's the closest I've come to lovin' a woman. We used to dance in her parlor. I taught her a few dances from my country—an Irish jig—she loved that one. I've never forgotten her. I think of her now and then to keep me goin', tellin' myself one day soon I'll go back and see her again."

Rufus stayed quiet. Jack got lost in thoughts about Lina and wondered how he could spend more than one afternoon with her or stolen moments in a barn. A memory of his father's angry, twisted face intervened. Jack shook the thought away. He had no business thinking of Lina on a long-term basis. He was as evil as his father. He would never subject a woman to the beastly way his father had treated his mother. Admittedly, he'd never had the urge to hit a woman, but he would never take the chance.

"Just a fool's dream," Rufus said. "A lady like Bertina was probably snapped up the minute I left. Nice dream, though."

On a turn of the road, Jack saw a dingy-looking house, small, with an overgrown yard filled with broken farm equipment. A dirty doll sat partially hidden in the tall grass.

"No wonder the horses are old and crowbait," Jack muttered. "Everything around here looks old and broken."

"Yeah," Rufus said. He knocked on the door.

After several minutes of rustling sounds and soft mutterings, an old lady with a withered face and a smile opened the door. Rufus opened the torn screen door and entered. Jack followed.

"Hello, Mrs. Waller. This here is my partner, Jack Palermo. We've come about those horses, ma'am." Rufus took his hat off.

The woman was petite and round; she wore a brown calico dress and a white apron. His mother had dressed the same, though as Jack remembered, the color of her dresses had faded after too many washings.

Jack hurriedly took his hat off. "Ma'am."

Mrs. Waller grinned. "Well, aren't you the handsome one?" The woman fluttered her eyelashes.

Jack smiled in spite of himself. The woman was old enough to be his grandmother.

"Now, I know you gentlemen want to see the horses, but I've prepared a meal for you, and a special sweet. Mr. McClintock really liked my cinnamon bread the other day. Did you, Mr. Palermo? I sent Rufus with a few pieces for you."

Jack nodded. "Yes, ma'am. Very good. Reminded me of my mother's baking."

"Well, isn't that sweet?"

She waved them forward through the crowded room filled with tables covered with knickknacks, glass figurines, and lamps. Why on earth did she have numerous lamps? She'd likely catch the place on fire if she lighted all of them. The kitchen was in better condition. The small round table was set with three bowls, utensils by each.

"Come, sit. I'll serve up the beef stew." Mrs. Waller bustled over to the stove. She also had a basket of cornbread in the middle of the table.

Jack ate every bite of the stew in his bowl. "Very delicious, ma'am."

"Thank you, young man." The widow smiled.

She put the dirty dishes in a tin basin of water she had ready. "Now, I know you didn't come here to visit. You want to see the horses." She ambled slowly through her obstructed parlor and grabbed a brown shawl from a nail, then led them out the back door, loose on its hinges. Maybe Jack could come by and fix things up for her.

The widow led them to the corral that also needed repair, where two horses, old and worn-out, grazed. With the Falwells so close, they needed to ride out fast. Jack doubted these sad-looking creatures could move. Their coats, however, were healthy. One was chestnut; the other was black with a white mark down its face. Jack liked that mare on sight.

"They are old, Jack, but they can do the job we need," Rufus said. "At least for now."

Jack nodded. "Yeah. You want sixty dollars for both, Mrs. Waller?"

She smiled. "Yes. I've had them for a long time." She patted the chestnut. "Hello, Jasmine. Say hello to Mr. McClintock and Mr. Palermo." She patted the black mare. "She's Snowdrop."

Jack frowned. He wasn't about to go around riding a horse named Snowdrop.

The widow laughed. "You can change their names, of course. I really hate to part with them, but I can no longer ride, and the boy I hire to help me with feeding them and with the more pertinent jobs I need doesn't come on a regular basis, only when he wants money for his nefariousness. Not the best worker I've ever had."

Jack's sympathy rose for the old lady. He decided to visit on Sunday and help her out. "Your yard needs to be weeded, ma'am. Varmints will make their homes in there."

"Don't I know? The boy, well, he says he doesn't have the tools."

"What the hell does he do?" Jack's temper flared.

"Jack, come on. Don't get riled. We'll take the horses, ma'am. Really appreciate this."

The widow gazed at Jack with a subdued expression. Jack hated to strike fear in a woman.

"I'm sorry, ma'am, to yell out like that," Jack said. He smiled to ease the frown he was sure was on his face. "Tell you what I'll do. Since you're giving my partner and me a bargain on these horses, I'll come back on Sunday and cut your yard. Do you have tools?"

"Yes, in the shed. I have an old scythe."

"All right, Mrs. Waller," Jack said. "I'll return on Sunday."

"Before you go, go to the barn and get the saddles. They're old, too, but I'll have no use for them," Mrs.

Waller said. "Since you're doing my yard, Mr. Palermo, it's the least I can do."

Jack realized the woman had her pride. She would accept work on her house in a mutual exchange. He thanked the woman. Rufus did, too. Once they'd saddled the horses, they said goodbye.

Rufus laughed as they rode back to town. "How do you like Snowdrop, Jack?"

Jack frowned. "I wish I could change the horse's name, but I can't. I wouldn't want anyone to come along and change my name. I'll call her Snow."

The soft chuckle Rufus emitted riled Jack.

Rufus shook his head. "Are you really going back on a Sunday to work on her yard?"

"Yeah," Jack said. "That boy takes advantage. If I find out who he is, I'm going to make him pay. Cheating an old woman like that."

"She has a lot of junk inside the house, too," Rufus said. "Liable to trip and brain herself and die alone."

"I wish she lived closer to town," Jack said. "Lina could send one of the orphans to check in on her now and then."

Rufus stared. "Well, look who's gotten all soft and sugary inside."

Jack frowned. "Hell, she could be my *abuela*."

"I hear you." Rufus rode in silence. "Not bad for two old horses, hey?"

"Not bad for two old men, either." Jack laughed.

"Stop saying I'm old," Rufus said. "You can be old if you want, but I ain't old." He muttered other words silently, then urged his mare to go faster.

Jack yelled and waved his hat and followed Rufus.

****

Lina had been trying for a couple of days to talk to Alejandro, but the boy avoided her as if he knew and nearly ran out of the room as soon as the lunch bell rang.

Today, she stopped him from leaving by asking him to stay for a few minutes before he left for lunch. He frowned, and she waited for his refusal, but he nodded.

She repeated the homework she'd assigned to the class. They put their supplies up and filed out of the room.

Alejandro squirmed in his chair.

"You're not in any trouble." Lina smiled.

The boy kept his eyes down.

Lina sat in a chair across from him. "I want to talk to you about your future."

"Future?" He glanced at her. "I have no future, Miss Lina. I'm going to survive any way I can, but I have no life to live. Maybe I'll be a gunfighter like Mr. Palermo."

Lina's stomach jolted. "You will do no such thing. You'll get into trouble with the law. You will always be running. What kind of life is that?"

The boy grinned, very unusual for him. He rarely smiled. "Adventurous. Exciting. The girls will like me."

"Girls do not like outlaws." Lina stood too fast and toppled the chair over. "Where did you get the idea girls like outlaws? Girls want a home, a husband, and children. They don't want to live outside, sleep on the ground, and be forever running from town to town."

"You like Mr. Palermo." The boy grinned again.

Lina tried to deny his statement, but couldn't. She straightened the overturned chair.

"Don't you?"

"We are not discussing me. We are talking about you." Lina decided enough was enough and she would turn this talk to the topic she wanted to discuss with Alejandro. "I'm concerned about you."

"You don't need to be," he said. "I'm fine. Maybe I'll get a job at the train. I've talked to the clerk. He says the railroad manager will go in next week."

"What kind of a job would you take?"

"Any kind. I'm not picky," he said. "I want to have money, rely on myself."

Lina nodded. "Very good. Excellent thinking. A boy, a young man like you, needs to think of a way to support himself. Maybe one day you'll want to get married."

"Married? Me? Naw, not me," Alejandro said. "Home and family like you want, Miss Lina? Not for me. I'm gonna be a loner." He paused and lowered his eyes to his desk. "I've always been alone, nobody to turn to. Er—well, only you and Father Pete and the nuns."

"They're my people, too, Alejandro," she said. "My parents died when I was twelve. I remember them now as if they were a dream. I was very blessed Father Bellamy took me in; he was the priest here before Father Pete. He was like a grandfather to me. He was in his seventies then, but he was the kindest, warmest man I've ever known. Father Pete is younger, so he's like my uncle, or brother, but he's still kind-hearted."

"He has a secret past," Alejandro said. She detected an imperceptible wink from the teasing boy. She hadn't seen the boy so playful before.

"What makes you say so?"

"Like you said. He's a young man. And he has a lot of book-learning. You can tell by the big words he uses. He could be a lawyer or a rich businessman."

Lina smiled. "You're right. I had noticed a

difference in him from a lot of men in Wylder. And I can see him in other occupations besides a priest. However, you should know, Alejandro, men become priests because they receive a calling from God, not because they choose the vocation to hide."

Alejandro frowned. The boy was still skeptical.

Well, he could be right. Maybe Father Pete did have a hidden past. But he'd been at St. Thomas's for a long time now, and she believed him to be the priest he said he was. Other than that, she couldn't say.

"I like you, Miss Lina," Alejandro said. "If I ever meet a girl like you, then maybe I'll get married one day." He grinned again.

"What's happened to you? You're different—happier."

"I've been thinking lately. Ever since we found Mr. Palermo. I heard he ran away from home when he was my age, and he took his little brother. Now, he wants revenge because outlaws killed his little brother. I want to have that kind of courage. I want to have such strong feelings for another person."

Lina nodded so he would go on talking.

"In going to mass and talking to Father Pete and the nuns, especially Sister Anne and you, Miss Lina, I've decided I want to make my mark in this town. I have a paper that says my name and the names of my parents. Some of these kids don't know that much about themselves. The nuns named them. I don't know who my parents were, other than having names, or what kind of work they did, or what they liked, so I can forge whatever kind of person I want to be."

"Of course you should make your mark. Make it a good one, Alejandro. No more talk about being a gunfighter. And I like how you used 'forge,' one of our new vocabulary words, in what you said." Lina grinned. "And thank you for liking me. I like you, too."

"But you like Mr. Palermo more." He jumped away from her hand to avoid her playful slap. He ran to the door of the room. "I don't know about you, Miss Lina, but I'm hungry as a bear."

Lina laughed as he walked out.

****

The moon was out, lighting the night. Jack knew he should go to sleep, but he wanted to go visit Lina. He missed her. However, he couldn't give her a future, and he couldn't risk getting further involved with her. He didn't want to leave her alone and with child. Lina deserved better. His life was possibly days from ending.

Why shouldn't I have a last happy moment in my life?

Lina would be happy, too. Such happiness would not last for either of them. Once they parted, the end would be imminent. His life would end in Wylder—or somewhere else—at the end of a rope. Lina's life would go on in Wylder, possibly saddled with his kid, unwed, alone and ostracized. Father Pete didn't strike him as an unforgiving man, given what he'd told him of his past, but he was also a priest, and the church followed certain guidelines. Jack couldn't take the chance on Lina losing her home, the only one she'd known for a very long time.

Rufus poked his head out of the cave. An hour after sunset he'd returned from working at the Widow Waller's house and crawled in to sleep. He'd learned carpentry along the way of his travels through many towns, and he'd offered to fix the old woman's doors. But he had told Jack he'd rather go after work in the grist mill, however tired. He refused to give up his Sunday's day of rest. He would get a good meal, so he didn't mind too much. "Shit, I'm tired," Rufus said now. "I could sleep through tomorrow."

Jack poured the dregs of his coffee on the ground. He didn't want to douse the fire. The chilly night air was creeping near. "You should. Not much else to do tonight. I'm getting mighty tired of waiting for those vermin to return. Maybe you're wrong. Maybe they already have the money and are on their way to who-the-hell-knows."

"Nope. I watched them leave after they shot you," Rufus said. "They hightailed it out of the churchyard like the devil was after them."

"Where do you think they stashed the loot?" Jack asked.

"Probably somewhere in the churchyard. Didn't have time to be choosy," Rufus said. "Any coffee left?"

"A little." Jack handed Rufus the pot.

Rufus grimaced as he took a swallow of coffee. "Damn. Another good thing about the widow. She makes a damn good cup of coffee."

Jack chuckled. "I'm tired of sleeping on hard ground. Maybe I'll ask Father Pete if I can sleep in the barn for a couple of nights. At least the hay feels different than cold, hard ground, and cold wind won't blow directly on me."

"Sure you're thinking of hay when you think of the barn?" Rufus laughed.

"All right, yeah, I want to see Lina, but I can't take the risk. For me. Or for her," Jack said.

"I get it," Rufus said. "Don't you wish we could stay…?" The man stopped. "Naw, forget it."

Jack understood what his friend refrained from

saying. They'd decided long ago not to dream of impossible things. They were outlaws on the run. They could never stop and set up even a hovel. They lived for the moments they had money and could pretend for a few days they had roots.

"I know, Rufus," Jack said. "This town, though, has—well, Lina, of course, but the feel of the town... Yeah, Wylder is still a rough place, but—a spark of hope?"

Rufus rapped Jack on the shoulder, not his injured one, thankfully. "Hope? What's that?" The man chuckled. "Yeah, I know. Goodnight, Jack. Can't stand to keep my eyes open."

"Goodnight."

Jack stayed in front of the fire and dozed off. He woke to find the fire had died out. Trying not to wake Rufus, he crawled into the cave and made his bed for the night, wishing he was lying on a soft bed in the orphanage with Lina.

****

Lina couldn't stop thinking about Jack. She missed him, and he hadn't visited. The few times she'd gone for a short walk around the town area she hadn't seen him. She returned to the orphanage sad and impatient. The restlessness had returned. While Jack was at the orphanage and during the few times she'd seen him, Lina had been happy. Her days had gone by faster.

Now, the days seemed endless. She'd been too forward. However, with a man like Jack, women probably fell all over him and he welcomed those advances. He'd found her lacking in some way. In all ways. She wasn't pretty, only average-looking, and she was an orphan who lived in a Catholic orphanage. What could be more boring?

Because her heart was filled with ingratitude, she told Sister Anne she was going to her room after class to reflect and pray. She stayed there, alternately kneeling and sitting, until suppertime arrived. Her thoughts had wandered more times than she cared to admit, but afterwards she didn't feel as restless anymore.

Jack had left Wylder bent on revenge. A man whose thoughts were preoccupied with killing another human being, even if he'd lost someone he loved to him, had no part in her life. She'd never be happy, or content, or at peace.

Most of all, Lina wanted peace. To a girl all alone in this world, the orphanage and the church filled her heart with serenity. If love had surfaced for Jack for a time, he had no permanent place in her life. She knew no other kind of life, and she didn't want to jeopardize what she had.

She sat with the nuns for supper and ate her modest meal. This was a time for reflection and prayer. She'd continue to participate in those activities, teach her class, and help her students. She was content with her life.

She helped the children to bed. Four girls in one room, the four boys in the other. She gathered them around her in the girls' room and read a story from the McGuffey Reader. Usually, she read from the Lenten reflections, but today, she took a risk and read them a secular story. Lina consoled herself with the knowledge the books catered both to a child's curiosity and the importance of religious values. Alejandro listened when she read stories from the reader.

When she finished, Lina told the boys to go to their room and get in bed. She'd go check in on them when she was finished with the girls.

"Miss Lina, will I ever learn to read like you do?" Hortencia asked.

The other little girls, all about the same age as Hortencia, looked at her with hopeful eyes.

"Yes, you will, Hortencia. All of you can learn to read very well. You've already succeeded with the first step. You want to learn. The next step is to practice and practice. Read all the time. Read as many books as you can find," Lina said.

Hortencia jumped up with joy. Lina put a stop to that. All she needed was for the girls to get exuberant. Whenever that happened, the boys soon joined in.

"Get in bed, all of you," Lina said.

She tucked them all in, blessed them with her rosary with the sign of the cross, listened to their prayers, and blew out the lamp.

"*Buenas noches, ninas.*"

"You said a no-no," Hortencia said. "You spoke in Spanish."

"Once in a while, we can."

"*Buenas noches,* Miss Lina," the little girls said.

The boys were harder to settle. Salvador wanted water. The other two had to go to the outhouse. And where in the world had Alejandro disappeared to? Rafael slept in a room off the kitchen to be close to the back door. A light sleeper, he would hear if anyone tried to sneak in or out.

Once she had settled the three boys down, Lina lit a small lamp and went in search of Alejandro. Where could he be? Maybe he'd been hungry, but she'd gone to the kitchen to get water and hadn't seen him. Surely, he wouldn't be in the classroom. He was not a devoted student. Lina hated to wake Sister Anne, or Father Pete. Where was that boy?

"Alejandro?" She whispered as loudly as she dared. "Alejandro?"

A cold blast of wind blew in, and the boy entered through the kitchen's back door. She turned and saw him there.

Rafael glared at both of them. "What's everyone doing up? *Vayanse a la cama.*" The boy waved his hand in disgust and went back to bed as he'd admonished both Lina and Alejandro to do.

"Sorry, Rafael. Alejandro, what in the world were you doing outside?"

"I have a message for you." Alejandro smiled. "Do you want me to tell you?"

"Of course," she said. "Does someone need help? We should call Father Pete."

"No, the message is for you," the boy said.

"What is it, Alejandro? At this late hour, don't play games." Lina almost stamped her foot.

"Mr. Palermo wants you to meet him in the barn tomorrow evening," he said. "He said he'll be busy all day."

"What?" Lina's heart thumped, and her cheeks heated.

"That's what he said." Alejandro grinned.

"He probably wants to tell me he's leaving," she said. "I thought he'd already left."

"Goodnight, Miss Lina."

Although Lina was embarrassed Alejandro knew about Jack, elation swept through her body; Jack had sent a message. She twirled with the lamp in her hand, almost dousing the lamp and spilling the oil. Sleep was impossible. She couldn't wait to see Jack. Maybe he would kiss her again, and hold her in his lap.

Chapter 9

Lina had been impatient all day and couldn't concentrate on anything. During morning prayers and mass, her mind kept wandering to Jack and how soon she would be with him. When she helped Sister Anne make breakfast, she kept dropping everything. The nun scolded her and told her to go to the dining room and line up the nuns and the children to go in and fill their plates.

She could barely eat the *atole*, a sweet hot beverage made with oats, milk, and cinnamon, and one of her favorites, especially in cold weather. Sister Anne frowned at her while they cleaned up and told her to keep her head on her duties and not on worldly and sinful things.

"Yes, Sister, I'm sorry," Lina said. The guilt rose up in her breast and reddened her cheeks. Sister Anne's frown didn't dissolve.

No classes were scheduled on Sundays. What would she do for the remainder of the day except wait for mealtimes, so she could help prepare and serve and clean up?

"My life is dull," Lina said. She glanced around the dining room, making sure all the tables were clean and trying to think of a task to do to make the hours go by faster.

"Dull is on occasion better in this turbulent world," Mother Superior's voice said.

Lina turned and bowed to the nun in charge. "I apologize, Mother. I spoke out of turn."

Mother Superior's mouth formed in a small smile. "You were by yourself, my dear. You didn't intend anyone to hear you. Except, perhaps God. However, I'm not certain how He can help you."

"I will be more grateful, Mother. I know I've been given many gifts," Lina said.

The Mother Superior was kind, but she was a person in authority and she sometimes scared Lina. Not because she'd ever been mean, or cruel, or said even one unkind word, but she was always so serene and peaceful. How did she accomplish utter calmness?

"Come sit," Mother Superior said and waved Lina to join her at the end of a long table. "I'm not judging you, child. My task is to lead the nuns, the children, and you to the right path. Yours is the final word. Tell me. What is troubling you?"

Mother Superior knew everything that happened in the church and the orphanage; she probably already knew about Lina's obsession with Jack Palermo.

Pushing through her embarrassment and shortcomings, Lina spoke. "Mother, remember when you advised me not to become a nun?"

Mother Superior nodded.

"You said I didn't have the calling, and I was very angry with you because I believed taking a vocation as a nun would help me to better serve God and people." Lina paused. "You were right."

Mother Superior didn't say, "I told you so." She never made anyone feel she was better or more important than they were. "What made you come to this conclusion?"

"You must know about Jack Palermo. The children and I found him shot, several weeks ago, at the end of the church property line."

Mother Superior sat quietly listening.

"I've had these feelings for him," Lina said. "I pray and pray and reflect so I won't fall into sinful thoughts, but the feelings return."

Mother smiled and took Lina's hand. "You are a young woman, Lina. You are meant to marry and have children. You are a very good teacher and take care of the children under your care, but as a woman, you want more. I understand."

"You do?"

Mother gave her small smile again. "I was a woman before I was a nun. I noticed young men. My vocation was stronger than my womanhood. Well, I'm still a woman, and I'm a mother to countless children who need me."

"I'm going to meet him tonight. He is busy all day, and he asked me. Should I?"

Mother stood. "The choice is not up to me. Be very careful, my dear. You know who and what Mr. Palermo is. And what he is not."

"He is not a man who will stay with me," Lina said.

"Bless you, Lina." Mother Superior turned and walked away, serenity still on her face.

Finally, after long, excruciating hours, and meals she barely tasted, Lina grabbed her shawl and mantilla and ran to the barn.

The cold wind blew at her. Hopefully, this didn't mean more snow. Was Jack already in the barn? The door opened wide when she pushed so she could enter.

"Jack!" Lina threw herself into his arms. "Oh, Jack,

it's cold. I'm glad you're here instead of in the cave."

His arms clasped her and held her close. "Me, too, Lina." He moved her a little away from him and kissed her. His warm mouth pressed on hers, and she responded with all the pent-up feelings she'd kept bottled in for days. Her hands caressed his body. Tingling sensations filled her from top to bottom, along with the heat of his body. She forgot the coldness of the night and the emptiness of her days until this moment.

"Come up to the loft with me," he said.

She followed him up the ladder. A blanket covered a corner of the loft, and he'd brought a small basket with food—baking smells floated up. A small oil lamp stood in a corner, "You brought food."

"Yeah," he said. "I worked all day with Mrs. Waller. She's a widow who sold Rufus and me a couple of horses. I cleared her yard, and she wanted to feed me as she always does whenever me or Rufus help her. Today, I told her I was going to meet a young woman. She packed a picnic for me."

"I think I like Mrs. Waller," Lina said. Her eyes raked Jack from head to foot. He grinned. She flung herself into his arms again. "I like you much better." She kissed him, and he responded. Before she realized, she was again on the blanket, and Jack was caressing her with his whole body. She grasped his wavy soft hair in her hands. "Oh, Jack, oh, I've missed this."

The movements changed. Jack pulled her shawl from her body and pulled the top of her dress down. His tongue caressed the cleft between her breasts. He wanted to bare her breast more, but her dress was one piece, with no buttons or laces, and it wouldn't go down farther. His hand moved down her body to the hem of the dress and pulled the garment up, and she was naked except for her camisole and bloomers.

"I'll be cold." Lina tried not to show her embarrassment as Jack removed her undergarments.

"I'll keep you warm," he said. Then he kissed her breasts, one by one, and caressed her body with his tongue, lips, and hands. She forgot her shyness. Her body began moving, and a feeling of warmth and sensation filled her.

How he managed to take off his clothes she never knew and was past caring. His bare hot body pressed against hers. She touched him slowly as languor overcame her.

"Lina." Jack kissed her, holding her face between his hands. "Listen to me, Lina. I want you to be sure before we do this."

"We're already doing it." She could barely breathe, and her heart thumped so hard, and her whole body ached for something she didn't know.

"There's more. I want you to be sure you want this."

"Yes, I do," she whispered. "I do." She kissed him.

"I'm leaving."

"I know." She hugged him closer. "I want to be with you."

Jack continued moving and caressing her body, kissing her lips. "I'm going to hurt you, but the pain will pass soon. I'll be as gentle as I can."

How could he possibly hurt her? This was so good, so warm and so…

She gasped and wanted to scream, but Jack pulled her face into his shoulder.

"Stay still," he said. "Let your body get used to me inside you."

Tears covered her cheeks. She kept her arms around Jack. Then, he moved slowly, and the warm feelings returned. Slowly, then faster and faster, he moved in and out. In the end, he shuddered against her. Lina held on tightly and smiled. She loved this man.

"I'm sorry. Next time will be better," he said.

"How could this get better?" Lina hung on. He kissed her cheeks and her lips.

"I promise. This will get ten times better." He handed her the dress. "I wish I could lie naked next to you, but it's too damn cold. Put this back on." Jack stood and put his clothes on. For a split second she saw his entire naked body—brown, muscular, and strong; she relished the knowledge she'd had him inside her.

Once they were clothed, they leaned against the wall of the loft. Jack held her close with a second blanket over them. She wanted to stay with him forever, a sentiment to be cautious about. She'd promised Mother Superior she'd be careful.

"Should we eat Mrs. Waller's picnic?"

"Yes, I am hungry," Lina said. "I ate all my three meals today. I'll commit a sin if I eat more, especially during Lent."

He grinned. "I think after what we did you'll be forgiven one more meal."

Lina laughed. "You're probably right. What did you bring?"

They both took out items of food—first the bread, and shredded beef with a tomato sauce she found was tasty.

"You'll have to ask Mrs. Waller for the recipe. This sauce is delicious." Lina licked her fingers.

Mrs. Waller had also packed cinnamon bread.

After they ate, they kissed, and soon they began to take their clothes off again.

"Are you sure, Lina? I don't want to hurt you. The first time can leave a woman sore," he said.

"I'm sure." He might leave her tomorrow. She would take tonight for herself. "Love me again."

He'd been so right. The second time was better. She'd flown around the barn and hadn't wanted to come back to earth.

Later, Lina, her arms around Jack, leaned on him and sighed. Jack kissed her at the back door of the orphanage leading to the kitchen. She hoped she wouldn't wake Rafael. He wouldn't appreciate being disturbed two nights in a row.

"Stay in the barn, Jack. It's too cold to walk all the way to the cave," she said.

"I will. But I'll be gone in the morning, Lina."

"I know."

He kissed her and opened the door, saw her in, and left. Lina's stomach dropped to her toes. She wouldn't dwell on tomorrow. She'd think about tonight.

****

Jack woke in the loft, and for once warmth engulfed him on waking. He kept his eyes closed as he remembered Lina with him last night. The softness of her body still seemed to be next to him. He wanted to keep this feeling with him for as long as he could. Once he left, his life would change. Falwell and Jenkins were probably riding back. They wouldn't leave a large amount of money behind. Revenge should be the only thing on his mind. Not now, though. He wanted to keep Lina close to him for as long as possible. Beautiful woman. Caring woman. A woman he could love if he had the time—and the choice. A woman he would like to wake up next to every day of his life. A woman he could never have—except for one night.

"Mr. Palermo? Are you awake?" A boy's voice asked from below the loft. Who the hell was he? He wanted to be left alone. He never dreamed. He'd stopped dreaming years ago. Had he ever really dreamed?

"Lina wants to know if you want breakfast."

Lina. She was thinking of him. That's why he loved her. Jack sat up. Past time to get back to the real world.

"No. I gotta git." Jack stood and pulled on his duster and slammed his hat on his head. He belted on his guns, grabbed the blankets and the basket, and climbed down from the loft.

"She sent breakfast anyway," Alejandro said. He handed the bowl to Jack. "Eggs, sausage, and tortillas. She wanted me to ask you if you wanted *atole*."

Jack grimaced. He hated the beverage, too sweet and thick. "No, thanks."

Alejandro laughed. "I feel the same way."

Jack sat on a bench and ate. He eyed the boy. "Don't get any ideas about using what you think happened last night to get money from me."

"Something happened last night?" Alejandro smiled. "I went to bed and slept like a baby."

I probably made a baby. Dammit.

Jack continued eating and frowning.

"You shouldn't eat when you're angry. Food doesn't go down well," the boy said.

"Kid, you don't know how many times I ate food when I was angry."

Alejandro didn't say a word.

Jack said, "Had to eat before my loving father

overturned the table because he didn't like what was offered."

"Is that why you ran away when you were thirteen? *Un monstro,* eh? I never knew my father. I barely knew my mother. Except for her singing and her smell. She smelled like Miss Lina, like a garden."

Jack glared at the boy.

Alejandro grinned. "I told Miss Lina if I ever meet a lady like her I'll marry her."

"Why'd you tell her that?" A jealous feeling overcame him, then shame. Alejandro was a boy.

"She wants me to find a trade to support myself and get a wife. And she doesn't want me to be a gunfighter like you."

"Wise words, kid," Jack said.

"But I do want to be like you." Alejandro turned away from facing Jack.

"Why in the hell for?" Jack set his plate down. "Look, kid…"

Before Jack could protest, Alejandro continued. "I don't want to be a gunfighter or outlaw, but I want to be like you because you're like the saints Miss Lina makes us study, like an avenging angel."

Jack picked up his plate and stopped before he took a bite. Alejandro turned to get the coffeepot. "I forgot Miss Lina sent coffee, too."

Fishing out his cup from his saddlebag, Jack poured coffee and drank.

"Nino, you are barking up the wrong tree. I ain't no saint and for sure not a damn angel," Jack said.

"I know, but you're a fighter like a saint. You're fighting for justice. Avenging your little brother. You make me want to make my mark on this world. You helped me get out of the sadness I was in because I'd been abandoned."

Jack continued eating and stared at the skinny kid. How in the hell could he see good in him?

"Hell, you were my age when you ran away with your little brother. That took courage, biggest courage I've ever heard of. I was abandoned. I hurt like hell for a long time, but later I was grateful not to be on the streets. I was in a warm place with food to eat, with people who cared."

"Hard shit to lose your mother, though," Jack said.

Alejandro nodded. "With Father Pete's help, I forgave my mother. She couldn't take care of me, for whatever reason."

"Why don't you sing? Lina wants you to," Jack said.

"Painful. My mother sang. She left me her guitar. I only played when the kids wanted to rehearse for you. I don't really know how to play."

"Learn. She left you her most prized possession," Jack said. "She could have sold it, but she left it for you. You can't ignore her gift."

Alejandro turned away, but not before Jack saw the tears in his eyes.

"I loved her. She was pretty, gentle, loving. That's why Miss Lina reminds me of her." Alejandro tried to give his usual grin, but he grimaced, and then he sobbed.

Jack watched him, helpless to know what to do. He pulled the boy into his arms. He'd hugged Jimmy when he was little and scared, or just plain needed affection.

"It's all right to cry, *nino*," Jack said. "I stopped crying when I was ten years old. I don't believe the choice did me a bit of good."

"Please don't tell anyone I cried like a baby,"

Alejandro pulled out a handkerchief from his pocket and blew his nose.

"What? What happened? All I know is you brought me a very delicious breakfast. Thank you. And thank the cook." Jack grinned.

Alejandro smiled and left with the dishes.

Jack sighed, remembered Lina, and wished he was a different man.

****

Lina whipped the eggs with the fork for scrambled eggs. She stopped and closed her eyes, thinking of Jack last night.

A sharp rap on the shoulder brought her out of her dream. "Hurry up and make breakfast. Didn't you get enough sleep last night?"

Lina avoided Sister Anne's eyes. "Yes, I did. I'm sorry." She dished out the cooked eggs from the pan and poured another whipped bowlful in.

Sister Anne harrumphed. "I'll bet."

Had she been seen? Would Alejandro have told anyone? She was surprised he'd been the one to give her Jack's message. Rafael was usually the one who delivered those, although the boy was surly and uncommunicative most of the time.

Lina lined up the nuns and children to be served and led the children to the tables in the dining room to eat. She wasn't very hungry, but she served herself a small portion of eggs on one tortilla, plus coffee. Memories of being with Jack resurfaced as she ate. He'd taken her virtue. What if she got with child? What would she do? Would Father Pete run her out of the orphanage? She'd sinned, a bad example for the children, especially for the girls. How could she stand in front of the class and expound on virtue and a chaste life when her stomach protruded?

Lina cringed as she ate her breakfast. She'd sinned, a very hard sin, but she couldn't feel remorseful, at least not yet. All she could remember was kissing Jack and touching him and the wonderful feelings he'd evoked in her, a wonderful and new experience. She smiled.

Sister Anne joined her at the table and harrumphed.

Lina tried not to meet Sister Anne's eyes.

"Don't think you're fooling me, Lina," the nun said. "I know how a woman looks after she's been with a man. Didn't I warn you? The man is going to leave you. If he doesn't get shot first."

Lina's heart jumped, and fear swept through her. "I pray not."

"What? That he won't leave you? That he won't get shot?" Sister Anne tore a tortilla in half with force.

"Both." Lina faced the nun squarely in the eye. She didn't know where she got the courage. Always unsure of herself, she'd never stood up to anyone before. *I love Jack.* Lina gasped. Yes, she did love him. Otherwise, she wouldn't have made love with him. She wished she could protect him from all harm. He'd been on his own for a long time. At least she'd had Father Bellamy and the nuns and then Father Pete. She had people to turn to, people who cared for her.

Tears filled her eyes. "I'm sorry, Sister Anne, to disappoint you after everything you and the church have done for me. I love him. I wish I could marry him and have his children. I know my wish is foolish. I'll probably have lots of regrets and much remorse in a couple of months. Right now, I want to dream a little. I want to pretend he's my Prince Charming, my hero, and that he loves me, too. I know how life really is, Sister. I've lived in an orphanage most of my life. Mine is not a life of dreams come true, but a life of hard work—and my faith."

Sister Anne ate and didn't speak. "You haven't disappointed me, child. I don't want you to feel the pain I did long ago."

"Pain is part of our life, too, Sister, as we both know," Lina said. She patted the nun's hand. "I'm glad you were here when I arrived. You were exactly what I needed—a caring person but who would take no nonsense from a bratty little girl." Lina grinned.

Sister Anne frowned. "You were a brat. Your parents had spoiled you."

Lina pushed the rest of her egg onto the tortilla. She was suddenly very hungry. "I make really good scrambled eggs."

Sister Anne rapped her on the shoulder again, but this time she laughed.

Lina laughed with her.

She helped with cleaning up the kitchen and then lined up the children to go to class.

Chapter 10

Jack had stayed away from Lina for a week now since last Sunday. He'd succeeded, but he couldn't get her out of his mind. All he could remember was spending time with her, enjoying the meal the widow had prepared. Most of all he remembered lying with her and making love with her. Contrary to her shapeless dresses, her body was as curvy as hell. He hadn't been able to see her naked, since the barn had been damned cold. Still was.

The freezing air hit his body through his duster. He couldn't stop thinking he'd taken advantage of her. He had no future here, or elsewhere. He planned to kill two men, and the law would be after him. And catch him. And hang him. She'd be an unmarried woman with a baby, accepted by no one. He feared the Catholic Church would turn its back on her, as by their rules intimacy came only after marriage.

He'd vowed to never make a woman miserable like his father had made his mother. Now he'd wronged her. He'd misled her and mistreated her. His heart leaped into his throat at the notion of never seeing Lina again, the shy, beautiful, but passionate woman. He could teach her. She could teach him, too. Maybe he could learn a gentler side of life with her.

Jack hit his head against the church. *Stupid idiot! Who do you think you're fooling?* He'd never lead a gentle life, not with his dark childhood and even darker present.

He did keep thinking of Father Pete's confession. Odd, how the priest had told him his story in trying to get Jack on the straight and narrow. The man did exude peace. For a moment as he'd spoken, Jack had glimpsed a way to have a better life. He'd wanted to make a good life for him and Jimmy, but he'd been too young when they'd run away. Jimmy had been practically a baby. Where could Jack have left him if he'd gotten work? They'd had to stay together. Then the Falwell brothers had loomed. Jack hadn't meant to stay with them too long, but sleeping on soft beds and having money to spend on food and clothing seemed a luxury Jack couldn't give up. Jimmy seemed happy, as well. Jack had tried to keep him away from the seedier side of the life he'd picked up, but deep down Jack had known staying with the Falwells would not be a good ending.

Jack decided he'd try to get one of the boys to take a message to Lina. He had to see her, if only for a few minutes. As he stayed behind the church, he saw one of the boys sneaking away from the orphanage to the next building.

Where is he going? Who is he?

Most of the children in the orphanage were little, four- to six-year-olds. Only Salvador and Alejandro were older. This one looked like Salvador, the shorter and plumper of the two. Alejandro was as thin as a board.

Jack decided to follow the scamp. He might be in trouble. Lina wouldn't forgive him if she found out he'd seen Salvador and hadn't tried to help.

The boy went in a straight direction from the orphanage. Once he'd gotten several feet away from the church, the boy slowed down. Jack slowed down, too. Again, the wintry air pierced his duster. He sure hoped this didn't mean more snow. Snow would delay his plans. And a snowstorm would probably delay the Falwell-Jenkins outfit from returning to town.

Jack stopped behind a clump of dried bushes and watched. Salvador had stopped by the tree where Jimmy had died and where he'd been left for dead. The boy walked behind another cluster of bushes and reappeared dragging a large sack.

Time to find out what the boy was up to. Before he could move, however, another boy popped out from behind the tree. Alejandro. *What in the hell?*

He heard Salvador's high-pitched voice, but the wind and distance carried the words away. Alejandro shook the boy. Salvador only hollered more and shook his head.

Jack decided to intervene and moved closer to the boys. "What's going on here?"

Both boys jumped as if they'd been scalded by hot water. They didn't say a word.

"What do you have there?" Jack looked behind them. In the dwindling light, he thought he saw a saddlebag.

"I found them. They're mine," Salvador said.

"You can't keep it," Alejandro said. "Is it yours?" He turned to Jack.

"Doesn't look like anything of mine," he said. "Is it a saddlebag?"

"Yeah," Alejandro said. "Looks expensive. Has the letters "F-O" printed on one side. Whose are they? Do you know?"

Jack realized the saddlebag must belong to the

Falwell brothers. Was it the money? "Have you boys looked inside?"

"It's mine," Salvador repeated and started to drag the heavy bags away.

"Money," Alejandro said. "It's not yours, Salvador. You'll get into trouble. We should turn it over to the sheriff."

Jack shook his head. "No. Too risky. The sheriff might think you stole it, at the least. At most, he'll ask a lot of questions you won't know the answers to, and he'll become more suspicious."

Were the Falwell brothers going to return here for the money? They were the ones who'd left their loot here. Maybe they should leave well enough alone. If the bags were gone, those *maldito* outlaws would turn to the church and the orphanage and everyone would be in danger.

"Jack, what is going on here? Salvador and Alejandro, you should be in your beds."

Jack turned to see Lina, covered with her mantilla on her head and a colorful shawl around her body. She shivered with cold.

"Lina, what are you doing out here? It's freezing. Could snow." Jack slapped his gloved hands together.

Lina frowned, looking at him with narrowed eyes. "Don't play innocent with me, Jack Palermo. I went to find you, Salvador, and you weren't in your bed. I didn't know you were out here, too, Alejandro. What are you up to? I will have to report you to Father Pete. You know his rule. You have to be in your bed by nine each night."

"Miss Lina, this bag is mine, and they…" The boy pointed to both Jack and Alejandro. "They won't listen to me."

"What is it?" Lina asked.

"The money stolen from the Bank of Cheyenne, if I'm not mistaken," Jack said. "That means whoever hid the stash here will come back. If they don't find their property, they may shoot up the orphanage."

Lina gasped. "What do we do?"

"I don't know," Jack said.

Lina stared at him as he paced around the area. "You do know, but you don't want to say. Tell me. What do we do? The main thing is to keep the children safe."

"You have to turn the money over to the sheriff. That way, word will spread that the sheriff has it, and the orphanage will come to no harm. They can't threaten you with anything if you don't have the money."

Lina wondered if that was the best thing.

Then she heard rustling.

Jack pulled out his gun.

Who is out there?

"Jack? You there, man?"

Jack laughed lightly. "Rufus, come on out, *amigo.*"

Rufus appeared, bent over, and lifted his hand as he breathed in and out fast.

"How come you're running?"

Rufus held up his hand as his rapid breathing continued.

"Are you running from the devil himself?"

"Not the devil, but close to. Falwell is headed this way." The man finally caught his breath. "I was at the saloon and spotted him. I hid in the crowd, but I heard him say the time had come to dig up the loot and hightail it out of Wylder."

Rufus took a deep breath. "They're not too far behind."

Jack glanced at Lina and the children. "Lina, take the children inside. These men are dangerous, and I don't want you in their line of fire."

"Will you be all right? I can get Father Pete to help."

Rufus said, "What's a priest gonna do?"

Jack smiled. "You'd be surprised. But no, tell him to keep everyone inside. I don't know what Falwell will do, and he has his brother with him." He turned to Rufus. "Did he have other men?"

"Nope, only Old Man Clemens," Rufus said. "He don't want to share, remember?"

Jack caught Lina before she left and kissed her. Her soft lips were warm and inviting. Her soft body beckoned him to stay close to her. But he couldn't. And he didn't know if he would see her again after tonight. "Take care of yourself."

"Jack?" Her troubled eyes pleaded with him.

"Go. Quick," he said. "I'll come to you if I can. If not, I'll get a message to you."

Lina nodded and hurried the children away. Salvador still claimed the bags were his.

"Let's pull the saddlebags back where they were," Jack said.

He and Rufus had barely finished when a man rode up. Jack didn't want to hide. Rufus wrenched him back.

"Jack, hold on, man. Listen to me. You can't just up and kill him with the law hot on their trail." Rufus held on as tight as he could to Jack.

Jack, though, was crazed, filled with revenge. He could taste blood in his mouth for the *pinche* son-of-a-bitch who had killed his little brother out of pure greed. "Let me go, Rufus, or I'll shoot you, too."

"Look what we have here." Bruce "Buzzard"

Falwell, wearing his top hat with a red feather under the band, spoke in a sing-song voice. "What in damnation? Rufus, you lowly sidewinder."

Buzzard. Jack heard the hated voice he hadn't been able to get out of his head ever since he'd come to in the orphanage, shot up and grieving for his little brother.

"What are you still doing alive, Jack?"

Jack spat on the ground and lifted his shotgun and aimed at the loathsome varmint in front of him. "Buzzard, you *cabrón*, the real question is how much time do you have left before you're lying cold on this earth."

Falwell must have heard the hatred in Jack's voice and the venom in his eyes, because he guided his horse back.

"Are you scared, Buzzard?" Jack moved the gun up and down Falwell's body.

Buzzard grinned. "No not scared. Funny how Jimmy ain't singin' too much now, is he?"

"My rifle has a special ballad written for you, *cabrón.*"

A sound of horses' hooves reached Jack's ears. Falwell took the opportunity and jumped from his horse and hid behind nearby bushes. Jack heard Jugbutt's voice.

"What the hell, Bruce? Whyn't you wait for me? This damn nag can't go very fast. Did you find the loot?"

Jack hid from Jenkins at Rufus' motioned suggestion.

Rufus walked out from the bushes and threatened, "I wouldn't make any sudden moves, Jenkins."

"Rufus, hell, you're alive?"

"Houston, get your ass over here." Falwell shot

toward the bushes where he'd seen Jack disappear.

Rufus ran for the bushes, too.

"What the hell is going on, boys?"

Jack heard an older man's voice—Old Man Clemens. "What kind of *pinche* reunion is this?" Jack was surprised he was still with the outfit.

"Shut up, old man," Falwell hissed. "We have to kill these sons-of-bitches." He shouted, "Where's my stash, Jack?"

"*Ala chingada* with your money, Buzzard," Jack yelled and aimed a hail of bullets toward Buzzard.

"Damn it! I'm shot to bits!" Buzzard yelped. "That's why I hired you to ride with us. You're one hell of a *pistolero.*"

Jack said, "Don't flatter me. You ain't gonna die yet, Buzzard. No, not yet. I want you to suffer."

Heavy fire ensued from the outlaw brothers.

Jack lunged up to head directly into the line of heavy fire.

"Hol' up!" Rufus held him back.

Buzzard yelled, "Clemons is hit. Dead."

Jugbutt said, "He's halfway to hell by now."

Jack's heart twinged at the loss of Clemons, but at the moment he had more pressing matters.

The sound of horses' hooves reached his ears. He peeked through the thick, dried-up bush. The sheriff and Father Pete rode up, the priest on the old donkey."

"You boys come on out," Sheriff Wylder said. "Slowly."

"You gotta be kidding, Sheriff," Bruce yelled. "We weren't born yesterday." He shot. The sheriff shot back. A yell sounded.

"Come out. Now," Sheriff Wylder ordered.

Jack heard movement in the bushes. The bastards were trying to run for the hills. He edged out of his hiding place and moved fast and fired a shot at Buzzard, who fell to the ground. The cock of a gun stopped Jack in his tracks.

"Drop your guns," Sheriff Wylder said.

"Dammit to hell." Jack let his guns fall to the ground.

A man yelled. Father Pete, still riding the donkey, hauled Jugbutt with a rope toward the animal. The priest jumped down and tied Jugbutt's hands to the horn of the saddle.

Then he helped the sheriff lift Buzzard like a sack over his horse. The man groaned.

The sheriff led all three men to the jail, with Father Pete's help. Jugbutt walked, his head down, leading his horse. Jack, following, looked back toward the bushes; he'd told Rufus to keep hidden and get word to Lina.

Hell. This hadn't gone like he expected.

Now he was on his way to jail and Buzzard was still alive. He'd get a chance again. He had to. This was the only way to honor his little brother and make his life count.

****

The sheriff had put Buzzard and Jenkins in one cell. He locked Jack up in the adjoining cell.

"Sheriff, my brother is still bleeding," Jenkins said. "Is the sawbones coming back?"

"You fixin' to bleed out, Bruce?" Jack taunted from his cell.

The sheriff spared them a glance before he drank from a cup. "Doc Sullivan already bandaged his wound. The bullet grazed his side. He'll be fine. The doc will be by later to change the bandage. You boys want coffee? A waitress from Jake's Place will be by soon with breakfast."

After the sheriff handed the men cups of coffee, he walked outside.

Buzzard said, "Wasn't anything personal, Jackie. Shit got out of sorts. When you ride with the Falwell-Jenkins outfit, there's bound to be bloodshed."

Jack hit the wooden wall of his cell. "He was my baby brother, you bastard. You should have made damn sure I was dead first."

Buzzard laughed without mirth. "I did, *cabrón.* Anyways, I thought I did. Rufus lied to me."

"By the way, where is he? Did we kill him?" Jugbutt asked.

"Hobble your lip, Houston," Buzzard said. "Did you ever think we'd end up in a hoosegow in blue northern-ass Wyoming? Hell, boy, when we found you, you could barely ride, let alone cross an *arroyo.*"

Old Man Clemens had been shot to death. Jack belatedly made the sign of the cross, wondering at the ease with which he remembered the motion. *Vaya con Dios, Viejo.* Must be the many times Lina had waved the cross over him.

"*Viejo* taught us how to *vaquero*, roping cattle and running them in cattle drives. All you did, Buzzard, was show us how to outlaw, *bandido cabrón*. Regrets, I have many. One is I won't lie cold in the ground in Texas. Second is when the devil checks who sent you home, my name won't be on your reservation."

Both Buzzard and Jugbutt laughed.

Jugbutt said, "We should've never left Texas. We had a time. We painted our noses a time or two."

Jack shook his head. "All that's over now, when you killed my brother. Besides, y'all could barely buy a beer, let alone a shot of tequila."

They were all going to hang. Jack didn't give a damn. An image of Lina rose up in his mind. Memories of Lina when he'd first seen her filled his head. He'd thought she was an angel. The memory of her in the barn, making love with such passion—she'd been an angel of another type. His heart ached, but he ignored the pain.

He heard Buzzard and Jenkins muttering. What the hell were they saying? *Shit. Didn't matter anymore.* Nothing did. Again his mind conjured up Lina. Jack closed his eyes to dim the picture, but Lina became more prominent in his mind.

Dammit it to hell.

Jack punched the wall.

Chapter 11

Lina opened the door to the jail, and she and Alejandro walked in.

"Here is the money, Sheriff," Lina said. Alejandro helped her get the saddlebags onto the desk.

The sheriff stood. "Where did you find it?"

"Alejandro found the bags, but he won't tell me where," Lina said. "Does it matter? Here's the money stolen from the bank in Cheyenne. Jack told us to turn it in."

The sheriff gazed at Lina, then examined the saddlebags, pulled out several bills. "Yeah, looks like the stolen money. I'll notify the sheriff in Cheyenne."

Lina glanced at the jail cells and saw Jack, smoking a cigarette. She hadn't known he smoked. He stayed seated on the cot and didn't glance her way. Her stomach dropped.

"Thanks, Lina," the sheriff said.

"What's going to happen to Ja-, to them?" She swallowed.

"I'm waiting on a telegraph from the sheriff in Cheyenne," he said. "These men stole the money from the bank there."

"We didn't steal no money, me and my brother." Buzzard stood at the bars of the cell.

Jack threw his cigarette on the floor and jammed his foot down. "You son-of-a-bitch. You're a murderer. You killed my little brother and you left me for dead. That's your real crime, *cabrón*. I want to live long enough to see you swing from the gallows."

Lina's heart beat faster. She'd never seen Jack this angry. Time and time again, when he was at the orphanage recuperating, he'd said he wanted revenge. However, she hadn't seen this rage in him before. His face darkened, and his eyes glittered with venom even when his glance flickered over her. Where was the man who had grinned at her and had brought forth secret urges she'd never known she had? Where was the man who'd been tender with her when he made love to her?

Alejandro stood in front of the cell where Jack was.

"You were right, Mr. Palermo, I shouldn't want to be like you," he said. "I don't want to hate."

Jack faced Alejandro. "Get the hell out of here, both of you. I don't give a damn what you think. I want revenge. Honor in death for my little brother."

Lina moved slowly to stand by Alejandro. Jack's eyes were red, his face contorted with hate. She couldn't see the man she'd known. "Revenge has nothing to do with honor. You will not feel anything but more profound loss when those you think are responsible for your brother's death are dead. You will be lost forever, too."

"You don't know what the hell you're talking about. Orphan or not, you don't know shit about the reality of life," he said. His eyes were devoid of any tender feelings.

Lina remembered him on their picnic. He'd smiled at her and teased her. He'd kissed her and had resisted taking her virginity because he couldn't make any promises. The man she stood before now was not that man.

"I know two wrongs don't make a right, Jack. You protected your little brother all your life. Do you think he would like for you to feel this much hate?" Her heart pounded, but she would not be afraid of him, though he was more frightening than anything or anyone she'd ever seen.

"You don't know a damn thing," he said.

"Did you fall in love, Jackie?" Buzzard laughed. "Is she the kind of woman you're consorting with now, Jack? Nuns? What happened to the more colorful women in your life?"

"Shut your *chingada* mouth, Buzzard!" Jack screamed, a primal yell. He pounded on the wall, as if he wanted to break the barrier down and kill the other man with his bare hands.

Both Buzzard and his brother laughed, and Jack kept pounding on the wall.

"Goodbye, Jack," Lina said, knowing he hadn't heard her, as angry and full of hate as he was at that moment.

She grabbed Alejandro's hand and pulled him away. "I will leave now, Sheriff Wylder. Good day."

Lina turned back, and Jack's bloody hand was spread on the wall. He still wore his long black duster, and his hair still hung down to his shoulders in a ponytail. Tears filled her eyes. She'd never see him again. Probably a good thing. What had Mother Superior said? *You know who and what Mr. Palermo is. And what he is not.*

In her naiveté, she'd romanticized their relationship. She emitted a light laugh. Not a relationship. He'd taken what she'd given because she was willing. She had seen him as her Prince Charming. She laughed again, but the pain piercing her body was not funny. Her heart had shattered into pieces.

Alejandro pulled her arm this time. "Let's go, Miss Lina."

Without looking back, Lina let Alejandro drag her along. Her leaden feet barely moved.

"You haven't disappointed me, child. I don't want you to feel the pain I did, so long ago." Sister Anne's words.

Outside, Lina looked up at the sky filled with soft fluffy clouds. She hoped the pain would subside soon, but as fresh tears ran down over the dried ones on her face, she feared this was only the beginning.

****

Jack was dreaming. He was in the barn loft with Lina, holding her naked body close to his. He held out his hand outside the covers, and the cold air penetrated. Sliding back under the cover, he caressed Lina's bare back, moving aside her silky black hair. He squeezed her.

"I love you, Jack," she said.

"I love you, too."

Then he heard a scream filled with pain, filled with hate. Jack saw Buzzard and Jugbutt, the two outlaws from the Falwell-Jenkins outfit. *Bastards.* They'd killed his little brother, and they would pay—with their lives.

He woke up on the floor.

"Hell, Jack," Buzzard said, the loathsome voice. "Shaddup. I'm trying to sleep."

Jack picked himself up from the floor and crawled back onto the cot. His chest heaved. A sense of heaviness settled on his chest. Then, he realized the harsh pain of loss was back—the pain of Jimmy's death intermixed with Lina walking out of his life yesterday. He hadn't thought he'd feel so much pain at seeing her leave him. Never before had the sight of a woman walking away touched him this way. Hell, he'd always been the one to walk away. No woman, no *person* had ever mattered to him as much as Jimmy—until now.

Sheriff Wylder handed him a cup of coffee. He took the offering without a word.

"Thanks, Sheriff," Jugbutt said. Buzzard echoed his thanks.

Pieces of shit. Think they have manners.

Jack wished he could go through the wall and punch the hell out of both *cabrónes.*

The door opened, and Jack's heart lifted; Lina had returned. However the man who entered wore a tan hat and tan uniform with a star—the star emblem of his much-beloved state of Texas, cut from a five-peso coin, pinned on his shirt. Jack remembered Miss Hildebrand had told him and Jimmy about the Texas Rangers history, including what they wore and the badges. Jimmy had been very interested in the badges.

This Texas Ranger's eyes held a glint of danger. His granite-hard face and muscular body convinced Jack he didn't want to meet this man in a dark alley, not even in a lighted one.

"Mornin', Sheriff. I'm Lewis MacArthur. We received a wire that you have two outlaws Texas has been wanting for a couple of years now." The Ranger tugged at the inside of his shirt and threw a paper on the sheriff's desk—a wanted poster.

"Wanted—Bruce Falwell and Houston Jenkins," the sheriff said. "They're wanted in Cheyenne for bank robbery."

"Texas wants them for murder," the Ranger said.

"What about Jack Palermo?" The sheriff pointed to the adjacent cell.

Ranger MacArthur glanced at Jack. "Don't know Palermo. Not in my jurisdiction."

"Whatta you mean, not in your jurisdiction?" Buzzard yelled. "He was with us throughout all those so-called murders."

The Ranger strolled up to the cell. Jack heard sliding steps as if Buzzard stepped back. "The only murderers I know about are you and your brother, Falwell." The lawman inched closer and took a deep breath. "Do you really want to argue with me?"

"Naw—sir," Buzzard said. "I don't. But I'm injured—got this wound. The doc says I can't travel."

The Ranger walked back to the sheriff. "That true, Sheriff?"

"Yeah, man has a gunshot wound. Doc says he can travel by Monday," the sheriff said.

"All right," the Ranger said. He pulled out another paper from inside his shirt. "Need you to sign this, giving me permission to take these *good-for-nothing bastards* with me to Texas."

The sheriff signed and handed the paper back.

The Ranger stuffed the paper back inside his shirt. "Gotta place I can stay for a couple of nights or three? How 'bout a saloon? A place to eat?"

The sheriff led him outside.

"Goddammit, Houston," Buzzard said. "We're done for. Might as well die right now. We're gonna hang for sure now."

"Hallelujah, Buzzard," Jack said. "Though I'd rather shoot you myself."

"*Chingado*, Jack. You're going down with us. You were part of the outfit for a long time. You gunned down as many folks as we did," Buzzard said.

"Nobody put my mug on a wanted poster," Jack said. "Must be 'cause I'm a *Mejicano*. I can be gunned down in the street. No questions asked." Jack laughed with no mirth.

"Dammit to hell," Buzzard said.

"What do you mean, Bruce?" Jugbutt asked. The man was always easily confused.

"Shaddup, Houston," Buzzard said. "Lemme sleep. Wake me when they bring breakfast."

Jack heaved a sigh. The two men he hated were going to hang. Didn't matter if Buzzard's wound healed or not. They were both going to die.

In three days the Ranger would take Falwell and Jenkins away. The sheriff had gone outside, and he didn't come back right away. The silence filled the room and Jack's heart. Buzzard and Jugbutt must have gone back to sleep. The elation he'd counted on feeling at their deaths didn't come. Instead, the remembrance of hearing Lina say his little brother was dead reverberated over and over in his brain. Lethargy filled him.

And there's another one, younger, but I think—he's dead.

Jack bent over his knees and held his head. His heart ached. He moaned. "Jimmy. Jimmy. Jimmy." He sank to his knees and turned to lean his head on the cot.

Lina's recent words to him also echoed in his mind.

You will not feel anything but more profound loss when those you think are responsible for your brother's death are dead. You will be lost forever, too.

Lina had been right. But what the hell did thinking

so help him? He had nothing now, not even the taste of sweet revenge.

****

The Saturday before Easter, Lina helped the nuns prepare for the celebration tomorrow. Saddened and dismayed because she had fallen in love with Jack, she still wished he could be in her life, but he was too full of hate. She didn't know how to help him feel differently.

Alejandro had told her yesterday that a Texas Ranger had gone to the sheriff's office. He had a wanted poster for the Falwell-Jenkins outfit. They were wanted for murder, and the Ranger was going to take them to Texas to hang for murder on Monday after Easter. What delayed the journey was one of the outlaws had a gunshot wound and the doc wouldn't release him until the injury showed signs of healing. Lina's heart had sunk to her stomach.

She poured the cake batter into the tin pan and remembered. Jack would hang. She'd never see him again. The last memory she would have of him was Jack in jail, full of hate, screaming with hatred and looking at her with no tenderness or emotion in his beautiful gray eyes. She gasped and covered her mouth to stop the sob. Taking a breath, she tried to slow her heartbeat and continue with her tasks.

A soft pat on her shoulder and a hand smoothing her back calmed her. "Child, do you want to take a break?" Sister Anne asked. She knew what had happened with Jack.

Lina continued to pour the batter. "No, Sister, I don't. We have too much to do. It's best if I stay busy. I'll be fine." She placed the tin in the oven and checked Father Bellamy's old timepiece for the time.

Sister Anne glanced at her with worry in her eyes.

Lina gave her a small smile. "I'm truly fine. What else do we have to do?"

Sister Anne shook her head but asked Lina to go check on the children. Since today was Saturday, there was no school, but they were in the classroom making decorations for the dining room and the fence outside. Lina walked to the classroom. The children rushed to her and greeted her. Many hugged her.

"What's this?" Lina's heart lightened with the affection she saw in the children's eyes.

"Happy Easter, Miss Lina," Hortencia said. The other children repeated the greeting.

"Happy Easter," she said. "Remember, though, this occasion isn't all about decorations and special foods."

"I know, Miss Lina," Salvador, jumping up and down, held up his hand. "I know."

"All right, Salvador," Lina said. "Tell us."

"The resurrection of Jesus," he said."

Lina smiled. "Correct. Don't forget. However, we also have to have fun because this is a happy celebration. What are you doing? Do you need any help?"

"We found sunflowers, Miss Lina," Hortencia said. "They're not very big. We're going to put them on ribbons and hang them from the chairs."

"I think that will look very pretty," Lina said. "One of these days we'll go outside again and search for more flowers." Lina remembered the cold February day when she'd taken the children outside for a walk and to name flowers they'd find when spring finally arrived. They'd found Jack and his brother. Lina's heart ached again and tears filled her eyes. She shook her head. Happy thoughts were all she would allow today.

"We also have ribbons," another little girl said. "A lady from town was here earlier, and she brought us a big box of all colors of ribbons." She pointed to the box.

Lina walked to the box. She fingered the many colored ribbons. These were used on ladies' hats. Maybe she could keep a couple for her colorless straw hat. She pulled out a green one and a yellow one and put them in her pocket.

Alejandro appeared at the door. "Miss Lina? There's a man to see you outside the kitchen door."

Lina's heart lifted.

"He's not Mr. Palermo, Miss Lina." Alejandro didn't smile.

"Will you please stay with the children and make sure they have everything they need?"

Alejandro nodded, concern in his eyes. He remembered her behavior the day they'd visited the jail. "Thank you. I'll return shortly."

Lina hurried to the kitchen. Who could this man be? She passed Sister Anne. "A man wants to talk to me."

Lina opened the kitchen door leading outside.

An older man stood outside dressed in brown rough clothing, holding a hat in his hand. He was Rufus, Jack's friend. She remembered him from the night they found the money.

"I'm Lina," she said.

"Yes, ma'am," the man said. He walked slowly toward her, clutching his hat in his hands. "Wanted to tell you, ma'am, that is, give you a message."

"From Jack? Did he send you?" Hope spread through Lina's body. He was alive. He hadn't been taken to Texas to hang.

"No, ma'am. I took it upon meself to come over and

121

let you know Jack is not in jail anymore."

"He's not? Where did he go? I thought the Ranger was taking him to Texas to—to…"

The cool breeze in the April morning made goosebumps on her arms. The sky still was as blue as ever and flowers were blooming, but Jack was going to be hanged. He was going to die.

"He's not going to hang. The Ranger had papers for Falwell and Jenkins, none for Jack. They're leaving on Monday, seeing as how Buzzard has a gunshot wound. I'm here to tell you the sheriff didn't hold Jack because the bank manager from Cheyenne was happy to get his money back. When the sheriff done told him it'd been Jack's idea to return the money, the bank manager…well, ma'am, he was satisfied. The sheriff let Jack go."

Lina's hope rose again, and her heart soared with happiness. They could be together—she and Jack. They could make a life together.

"Is he with you? Tell him to come tomorrow for the Easter celebration, Tell him…"

"He's gone, Miss Lina," Rufus said. "I couldn't convince him to stay. He says he's no good to anybody. We's going to Colorado, New Mexico territory, away from here. That's all he said. I'm meeting with him outside of town."

"Oh." Lina's heart broke into more pieces. "Oh—er—well…" Tears filled her eyes. "I know he's very angry, full of revenge. He wouldn't be happy here, where he met those men he wanted revenge on and he couldn't kill them himself." Her throat hurt with the pain of holding back her tears. "Th-th-thank you for coming to tell me, Rufus. Do-do-do you-you…" Lina cleared her throat. "Do you need food for your journey? We…we…made bread, and we have a lot of food for tomorrow's celebration. The town's merchants have donated…"

"We're fine, ma'am. Jack is over at the widow's house, and she's preparing food for us. Thank you anyways. I best get going."

Lina took her rosary out of her pocket and walked up to Rufus. She made the sign of the cross on him. "May I have your hand, Rufus?"

Rufus held out his open palm.

Lina made the sign of the cross over the palm of his open hand. She closed it. She raised her face to the man. "Will…will you, pl-please give this prayer to Jack? Tell…tell…him that I wish him…well…and that I will ne-never forget him."

"Yes, ma'am, I will," he said and placed his hat back on his head and climbed on his horse.

"I wish you well, too, Rufus. Take…take care of-of each other." Lina couldn't bear the pain another minute. She ran inside and didn't stop until she fell on her bed. Sobs wrenched her body. She would never see him again. Never again.

Chapter 12

Lina stood outside in the field behind the church for the sunrise Easter mass. She wore a light green dress and her hat with the green and yellow ribbons she'd threaded through it. For one day, she would be colorful.

Father Pete had begun the service in the pre-dawn hour. As the mass ended, the sun rose in the east. Tears filled Lina's eyes, both because of the beauty and solemnity of Easter and the sunrise and because of the sadness she lived in since Jack left.

The children's voices brought her back to the tasks of the day. She led them inside the kitchen to the dining room. She'd helped the little girls put ribbons on their hats. The girls had white dresses to wear; the boys wore white shirts instead of their everyday gray tunics. Washing day would be an arduous task, but Easter had come.

Breakfast would be served, and then the festivities would begin. The children jumped up and down with excitement. Lina allowed them for once. The orphanage seldom had enough food or time to let the children truly enjoy a day.

Lina hadn't slept well last night. After she'd cried herself out, she washed her face and resumed helping the nuns with the preparations. She and the children had a playful time hanging the ribbons and the sunflower wreaths they'd made.

She wasn't very hungry, but today promised to be a long day. She'd better eat. The children, wide eyes filled with excitement, took the nuns around and showed them the decorations they'd made. The colorful ribbons swaying every time the little girls moved their heads added to the festive occasion.

Once breakfast concluded and Lina had assisted with cleaning the kitchen and the dining room, Father Pete entered the kitchen and said everyone had done a great job and made the Easter celebration glorious.

"Lina, will you come to my office for a few minutes, please?" he asked.

Sister Anne frowned. "We have to get the children ready for the games."

"Will you please get Sister Beatrice to start them? I won't take too much of Lina's time."

"Yes, of course, Father Pete," the nun said.

Lina shrugged and lifted her hands palms up, indicating lack of knowledge of the priest's motives.

Inside Father Pete's office, he motioned for her to sit on a wooden chair in front of his small desk. He sat in his chair and smiled. Lina's heart beat fast. What could he want? Had he found out what she and Jack had done and would ask her to leave?

"Don't worry, child," he said. "I think you'll find this is good news." He pulled an envelope from under a pile of papers and books. "The sheriff came to see me after the church service, and he said the bank's stolen money was found on the church grounds and you had returned it."

Lina's nervousness subsided a little. "Yes."

"The bank offered a reward for the returned money. The sheriff said since the money was found on church grounds, the reward belongs to the church."

Lina nodded. "I agree. The church and orphanage need more than the monthly allowance to survive. With a little extra money we—I mean you—can buy more supplies and books for the children."

"The reward is quite substantial—two hundred fifty dollars," the priest said.

Lina jumped up and clapped her hands. "Oh, Father Pete! Oh, my! A miracle!"

The priest clasped his hands together and closed his eyes. "Lina, you are a blessing to this church."

"Thank you, Father." She smiled, but she didn't know why he would tell her such a thing. She waited.

"The reward is for you," Father Pete said.

Lina frowned. "For me? No, the money is for the church, for the children."

"The sheriff said you and Alejandro had taken the money to him," the priest said.

"Yes, we did. But we're both part of St. Thomas, so the money belongs here."

"Listen to me, Lina. You've been here since you were twelve years old. Now, you're twenty-two. You're a young woman and one day will get married. This money can help you in your new life."

"Oh, no, Father. I will never get married." Lina glanced down at her hands.

"I understood from Sister Anne you met a young man, Jack Palermo, the gunfighter."

"Yes, Father. Well, I helped take care of him while he recuperated. We went on a picnic once, here on the grounds. He left yesterday. His friend told me they were going very far, Colorado, maybe."

"I'm sorry." The priest picked up the envelope.

"Whatever the case, this reward money is yours, and no arguments."

Lina didn't know what to do. She must speak to Sister Anne.

"Tell you what. I'll keep it here in my desk, locked up. When you decide, the money will be here for you."

"Yes, I think that would be for the best."

Father Pete stood. "Let's go enjoy the rest of the day."

****

Lina found the children in the middle of the foot races, where Sister Beatrice told her no one could find Salvador. Lina helped Sister Beatrice with the games.

Before long, Sister Anne, a scowl on her face, walked up with Salvador in tow. "The boy decided climbing up a tree was the best hiding place," she explained. She turned to the culprit. "Finding you took an hour. I've a good mind to send you to your room and make you miss out on the rest of the celebration, you naughty child."

Salvador glanced at Lina. "Miss Lina, you said this was a celebration. I can't miss out, can I?"

"Sister Anne has to decide, Salvador," Lina said.

The nun laughed. "Oh, go on, but you…"

Salvador ran off before Sister Anne finished speaking. The rest of the boys, of course, wanted to climb trees after that.

She shook her head. "Children. Well, come on, Lina, let's go get the food ready. What did Father Pete want with you?"

After Lina told her, Sister Anne hugged her. "Oh, my dear child, I'm so happy for you."

"I can't accept the money, Sister Anne. The reward

belongs to the church. I have no use for it. However, Father Pete insisted, so I'll help the church." Lina smiled.

The nun put her arm around Lina. "Your decision, my dear. Let's get to work."

The bell for lunch sounded, and Lina lined up the children to go inside, wash up, and sit down for the second meal of the day. This was the special one—with shredded beef donated by Finn Wylder from the mercantile, baked bread, and all kinds of canned vegetables—peas, carrots, corn, and pinto beans. Lina's mouth watered at the bounty of good food. Her appetite had returned after the exertion of running after the children during the games.

Once the children were served, they took their plates to the tables they had set up outside. Blankets on the ground had also been spread out and secured with rocks at each corner. The wind could come up at any time and take away anything not pinned down.

Father Pete said grace, and everyone begin eating. Lina sat at a table with Sister Anne, Hortencia, Alejandro, and a few of the nuns. She'd finished her meal and was going to take her empty plate inside and get more lemonade when she saw Alejandro wave to her.

"Miss Lina?"

Lina smiled. "What is it, Alejandro? Did we lose Salvador again?"

"No, Rufus is here, in front of the church. He wants to talk to you," the boy said.

"What? Yesterday, he told me he was leaving." In spite of telling herself countless times she would forget about Jack, a glimmer of hope filled her.

Alejandro shrugged. "Go talk to him."

Lina handed her plate to Alejandro and ran around

to the front of the church. She saw Rufus, this time dressed in blue dungarees and a red shirt with a black bandana around his neck.

"Rufus?" Lina's heart pounded. "What are you doing here? You—you—left, I mean…"

"Miss Lina, I convinced Jack to come talk to you, if you want to talk to him, that is." Rufus gave her a small smile and fiddled with his hat. "Do you want to talk to him?"

"Yes," Lina said, not caring if she sounded over-eager or naïve or silly.

"He's over there by the tree where the outfit left him and Jimmy for dead," Rufus said. "I'll be going now."

"No, Rufus, please stay." Lina caught his hand. "Come back around with me. We have food. We're having a celebration. Please."

Lina took Rufus to Sister Anne.

"Sister Anne, this is Rufus—uh…" She didn't know the man's last name.

"Rufus McClintock, ma'am." He held out his hand to the nun, who took it.

"Will you please fill a plate for Rufus? Give him anything he wants." Lina kissed the man's weathered cheek. "Thank you, Rufus." She ran toward the tree—and Jack.

"Lina, where are you going? Where is that girl going?" Sister Anne's words barely penetrated Lina's ears. Jack had come back.

She reached the tree but didn't see anyone. "Jack? Jack, are you here?"

A rustling sounded from the nearby bushes. "Hello, Lina." Jack stood before her, wearing black pants and a white shirt buttoned to the neck, where he had tied a black shoestring tie. He held his black hat in his hand.

Lina couldn't speak. He looked so handsome. Was he really standing in front of her?

"You're beautiful. I wanted to see you wear a color besides gray," Jack said.

Lina swallowed. "You're very handsome."

Jack grunted. "Ah—I was going to leave, but—um—that damned Rufus wouldn't stop yakking about the big mistake I was making in leaving you behind. I was ready to take my rifle out and shoot him."

Lina gave him a small smile. "I'm glad you came back. We're—we're having a celebration—for Easter—there's lots of food. The children are all dressed up, a little dirty now after playing games, but…" Tears filled Lina's eyes. "I'm glad you returned. Did you come to tell me goodbye? You can stay to eat, can't you? Rufus is eating now."

Jack put his hat on a branch of a bush. "I came back to tell you I did make a mistake in leaving you behind—hell, in plain leaving. You were right. After the Ranger told the sheriff Falwell and Jenkins were going to Texas to be hanged for murder, I didn't feel as happy, or as avenged, I guess, as I'd thought I'd feel."

Lina waited, aching to be in his arms. All she wanted to do was tell him she loved him and to please stay with her.

"I came back for you," he said. "I want you in my life." Jack cleared his throat. "I need you in my life—your goodness, your optimistic way of looking at life, your—love. I love you, Evangelina Gaitan. Will you marry me?"

"Oh, yes." She ran into his arms. "Yes. Yes. Yes. I'll be in your life. I'll marry you. I love you."

Jack held her close and squeezed her.

"I don't know where the hell we're going to live, but…"

"I don't care if we live in a cave," Lina said. "We'll be together. We'll make it work."

"We don't have to live in a cave, but we might have to live in a barn for a spell," Jack said. "Mrs. Waller, the widow Rufus and me have been helping, has land she can sell to me, but I have to work to get the money before I can…"

"I have money," Lina said.

"What?" Jack frowned.

"The sheriff gave me the reward for returning the bank's money. We can buy the land now. I also want to help the church and the orphanage. I have two hundred and fifty dollars. That will be more than enough, won't it?"

Jack didn't say a word; he stared at her as if she'd grown two heads, and then he frowned.

"I won't have my wife take care of me," he said. "I can take care of my woman. I will not be a *mantenido*."

Lina's heart skipped a beat. Her fear and hesitance returned. She steeled herself to speak. The next minutes were crucial to how the rest of her life—with Jack—would be. She took a deep breath, took his hand.

"You will still take care of me and the children I hope we'll have. We'll take care of each other and our family, Jack. Think of the money as my dowry."

"Your what?" Jack's stance was rigid.

"Many of the ladies in town are here from the eastern United States, and a few of them are from England. They're rich ladies. They talk about marrying their husbands to help them rebuild their houses, or pay their debts off. Why shouldn't our marriage start the same way?" Jack remained silent. He turned away from her.

"Jack?" Lina's stomach sank. He was going to leave her again. She shouldn't have spoken about the money. Her decision had already been made to let the church have it. Why had she opened her big mouth?

Finally, he faced her. "I'm behaving like my father, yelling out orders, demanding I'm the man of the house. His way made me and my family miserable."

Lina observed the struggle on his face. Slowly, his body relaxed, and he smiled. "I'm glad I met you, my darling, sweet Lina." Jack pulled her close to his body and hugged her.

She sighed and held tightly to him. "I'm happy I met you, too, Jack."

"I can hear him singing again," he said when he released her.

"Who?"

"Jimmy, my little brother. I always remembered his singing, but while I was bent on revenge, I couldn't hear him. In the jail, you asked me if he would be happy to see me filled with hate. He wouldn't. The best way to honor my little brother is to stop thinking of revenge and to stop wishing I'd died instead of him."

Jack took Lina in his arms and hugged her close. Guitar music sounded in the distance. They turned to see Alejandro walking toward them playing his guitar, and he stopped and waved at them to join in the celebration. The children, colorful ribbons flying in the air, ran toward them.

Lina laughed. Jack kissed her, and his kiss was a promise, a promise they made to each other, to love each other from this day forward.

A word about the author...

L. M. Gonzalez writes about the loves and lives of women and the challenges of romance. Her stories, set against a backdrop of strong Latino culture blended with an American lifestyle, are refreshing and capture the essence of everyday Hispanic life.

Visit her at:

https://lmgonzalez.wordpress.com/

Thank you for purchasing
this publication of The Wild Rose Press, Inc.

For questions or more information
contact us at
info@thewildrosepress.com.

The Wild Rose Press, Inc.